JUST DREAMS

Greer thought she was escaping the demands of running her London-based business for the peace of the Welsh countryside. Instead, she encountered Byron — a man sometimes baffling and infuriating, but always intriguing. It was a relationship overshadowed by events in the past, which even she couldn't control, any more than she could harness her own emotions where the dominant Welshman was concerned — even though he had told her that he was 'not available'.

Books by Marigold West
in the Linford Romance Library:

TRUTH TO TELL
ECHOES OF ANOTHER LOVE

SPECIAL MESSAGE TO READERS

This book is published under the auspices of

THE ULVERSCROFT FOUNDATION

(registered charity No. 264873 UK)

Established in 1972 to provide funds for research, diagnosis and treatment of eye diseases. Examples of contributions made are: —

A Children's Assessment Unit at Moorfield's Hospital, London.

•

Twin operating theatres at the Western Ophthalmic Hospital, London.

•

A Chair of Ophthalmology at the Royal Australian College of Ophthalmologists.

•

The Ulverscroft Children's Eye Unit at the Great Ormond Street Hospital For Sick Children, London.

You can help further the work of the Foundation by making a donation or leaving a legacy. Every contribution, no matter how small, is received with gratitude. Please write for details to:

THE ULVERSCROFT FOUNDATION,
The Green, Bradgate Road, Anstey,
Leicester LE7 7FU, England.
Telephone: (0116) 236 4325

In Australia write to:
THE ULVERSCROFT FOUNDATION,
c/o The Royal Australian College of Ophthalmologists,
27, Commonwealth Street, Sydney,
N.S.W. 2010.

MARIGOLD WEST

JUST DREAMS

Complete and Unabridged

LINFORD
Leicester

First published in Great Britain in 1990 by
Robert Hale Limited
London

First Linford Edition
published 2002
by arrangement with
Robert Hale Limited
London

British Library CIP Data

West, Marigold
Just dreams.—Large print ed.—
Linford romance library
1. Love stories
2. Large type books
I. Title
823.9′14 [F]

ISBN 0–7089–9944–1

Published by
F. A. Thorpe (Publishing)
Anstey, Leicestershire

Set by Words & Graphics Ltd.
Anstey, Leicestershire
Printed and bound in Great Britain by
T. J. International Ltd., Padstow, Cornwall

This book is printed on acid-free paper

'I suppose I must thank Penoyre — without you there wouldn't have been the need, or the determination.'

1

Greer watched the water as it dripped relentlessly from the hole in the roof into the bucket. Everything in the cottage felt sticky with damp, and the windowpanes were misted up — she could scarcely see the drenched trees that crowded round the grey stone walls.

'And to think,' she spoke aloud to herself, her voice sounding small and tinny in the sloping-ceilinged room, 'I came here to get away from all the hassle!' She grinned wryly. 'Out of the frying pan into the fire, as usual.'

Feeling distinctly tacky without having had a bath, she descended the stairs and left the cottage with a feeling of relief. Outside, the day, though still drizzly, was muggy, and she felt overdressed in her colourful Aztex sweater. The temperature inside the house must be ten degrees lower — it could be remedied, of course, by a blazing log fire, if only there were any logs.

Ah well, all these ills will be cured once I've found a phone-box, she thought, and belted herself into her car with a feeling of delight at returning to the familiar, with everything in working order and, above all, clean!

With her stereo blasting out her favourite Stevie Wonder track, and the powerful engine responding to the pressure of her right foot, she felt better already. Though definitely not prepared to forgive the sins and omissions of the letting company or, more specifically, the owner of the semi-derelict property she'd regrettably rented for her holiday.

The lanes, though narrow and made blind by thick, high hedges were fortunately, given the speed at which she drove, deserted. The odd horse gazed mournfully over a gate, its mane tangled and wet, and an escaping sheep caused her to brake sharply and the offending animal to leap for shelter into a ditch, bleating with indignation.

The rain seemed to have renewed its serious intent by the time she reached the crossroads, and she had to make a quick dash across the sodden grass verge to the shelter of the solitary kiosk she'd vaguely noticed the night before. Taking a piece of paper from her pocket, she uttered a short, mirthless laugh.

'Country Idylls' ran the legend, and she remembered how much she'd looked forward to her 'escape' from civilisation, before disillusion had set in.

Greer stabbed the number. The phone rang . . . and rang . . . and rang, and her irritation mounted as she read 'If you have any problems, contact the owner of the property, Mr B. Meredith.'

'Huh! Problems? The place is a joke.'

At last a lilting Welsh voice responded. 'Hello, Bethan Meredith here.'

Greer bit off an angry expletive. '*Mrs* Meredith? I believe it's Mr Meredith I need to talk with.'

Again — she waited, trying to put a lid on her simmering temper, whilst Mr Meredith was obligingly fetched.

'Who is it?' The voice startled her momentarily, with its depth and resonance, and yet with a melodic intonation that was strange to her ears.

'Greer Jameson,' she replied economically, but the waiting silence indicated that he hadn't the faintest idea who she might be. 'I arrived last night at 'Ty Bach'. I've rented it for a month.'

'Oh yes!' He was evidently a man of few words.

'Well, it's a disgrace! There's water coming through the roof in at least two places — I've only been there one night and yet my clothes already feel damp. I'll probably get rheumatism from sleeping in the bed there — which, incidentally, is so lumpy you need to be a contortionist to get comfortable in. The gas cooker doesn't work, and the place is freezing.'

She spoke with biting fluency, but the only response she elicited was a deeply heartfelt sigh.

'I can't imagine,' she continued, still on the attack, 'how you can let such a property. Perhaps some people aren't accustomed to a decent standard of living, but I can assure you that I am and, in my estimation, living in your cottage for a month would be intolerable. Now — what do you propose to do about it?'

'If you'll let me get a word in edgeways.' The man actually sounded amused at her dilemma and Greer practically breathed fire down the line. 'In the first place, most people relish the lack of modern conveniences in the country — '

'By modern conveniences you mean a cooker that works, a fire . . . there aren't even any logs to burn!' Really, the smugness of the man was unbelievable!

'As for the cooker, did you turn on the tap on the gas bottle?' At her uncomfortable silence he sighed expressively. 'We're not on mains gas here, and there's a bottle under the sink. Logs are in the barn at the back, behind the old tractor. Any good at lighting fires, are you?'

'I'm a reasonably practical person, yes.' Greer seethed through clenched teeth. 'I suppose you're about to suggest I get up a ladder and patch up the roof? Then I'll draught-proof the front door and nail down the floorboard in the bedroom that's so loose it nearly sent me flying through the window.'

'No need to do all that. Not woman's work, is it?' She suspected he was enjoying himself at her expense. 'But if your husband's keen on DIY, well, I wouldn't mind, indeed. Could occupy his entire holiday.'

Greer held the receiver away from her ear and looked at it as though about to do it actual physical harm. I'll sue him, she thought.

'If I had a husband, which, fortunately, I don't,' she began, breathing hard, 'I wouldn't — ' but at that point her last ten-pence worth ran out, leaving her to glare at the impotent instrument as it burr-ed away contentedly to itself.

There was nothing for it but to find a shop for a few basic necessities and decide on the best course of action.

Driving back, the rain was horizontal, great waves of it sweeping across and defeating the windscreen wipers. She peered through the blur of water, wondering how she'd managed to find the place at dusk, when every hedge, every gate, looked the same.

At the last minute she spotted the narrow turning and swiftly spun the wheel, only to realise, too late, that it wasn't the turning, just the muddied entrance to a field without a gate. She braked hard, and put the car into reverse.

The wheels spun, the engine shrieked, and she remained exactly where she was.

Her car, her much-prized, hard-won,

normally gleaming Volkswagen Scirocco, was stuck fast in oozing mud. Off a road that led to nowhere. In the middle of a cloudburst.

For someone who'd built up something of a reputation for being in control of her life, she wasn't doing too well. Her chestnut-brown Kurt Geiger boots sank instep-deep into the churned up, rich-red Welsh mud as she left the car, and the unrelenting rain threw itself at her face and reduced her smooth blonde tresses to a soaking, clinging mess.

There was one, very small, consolation.

She could just discern the outline of the cottage over the next hedge. In her present state, even that was a haven.

She ran, against the sheeting rain, up the short incline to shelter.

Gasping for breath, Greer staggered into the hall and leant back against the door in relief at the sudden calm.

But only for a second.

A muffled sound from above told her

she wasn't alone in the house.

Her heart did a backward somersault as she heard footsteps above her and she realised whoever it was couldn't have helped hearing her crashing back indoors.

And wasn't afraid of discovery.

Greer stared up the shadowy staircase. The thought of running back out into that weather was almost less enticing than facing an intruder.

Before she had time to move, though, the outline of a large figure blocked out what little light came from the grubby skylight. He looked down at her, silently.

'You've got two minutes to get out before my husband arrives with our German Shepherd.' Greer was thankful that her well-practised ability to think on her feet hadn't deserted her.

Heavy booted feet descended the creaking stairs.

Greer waited, her heart beating a tattoo, until the metal tips clattered on the stone flags. Even if she'd taken to her heels, given the length of the man's legs, he'd have caught her in a few strides.

He loomed over her menacingly.

This shouldn't be happening here, a part of her mind was thinking. London's supposed to be the dangerous place, yet I haven't been here five minutes and I'm faced with what I can only presume to be a burglar.

He did nothing. Just stood while she stared at him apparently fearlessly. If she kept calm she might even yet stay in control of the situation.

The intruder was well concealed in a hooded jacket with a flap covering the lower half of his face. Damp, dark hair clung to his forehead and the thought occurred to her that she'd have difficulty in identifying him later, if it should come to that. Except, perhaps, by his striking height and the exceptional breadth of his shoulders.

She jumped when he finally spoke.

'Fortunately,' he laid heavy stress on the word, 'you don't have a husband.

Nor, I imagine, a German Shepherd.'

'Oh yes I have,' Greer asserted, her chin high and brave. She waved a hand vaguely in the direction of the front door. 'And the dog's as vicious as can be — ' She broke off and stared as the man gave a muffled laugh.

A new fear took hold of her. He must be mad, as well as powerful. Even she couldn't cope with that combination. 'I'm glad you're amused, though I can't see any humour in the situation.' If she kept talking maybe he'd take fright and go. 'Nor will you, when the dog's teeth are sinking into your leg.'

Her eyes widened as the man began to unbutton the flap that concealed his face. If he wasn't concerned at her seeing him, that could mean only one thing. She could feel her grip on her fear slipping away and almost panicked, looking around wildly for a chance to escape.

'By God, but you've a vivid imagination!' His voice, unmuffled now, was faintly familiar, and her gaze shot back to his face.

It was one she was certain she'd never laid eyes on before. It wasn't the sort of face one would forget in a hurry, even seen in the half light. A dense but carefully shaped beard followed the strong line of his jaw and a wide, determined mouth. Darkly defined eyebrows rose above cynical eyes of an unexpectedly clear blue. Not the blue of Greer's sunny, summer-sky blue eyes, but the deep, solid blue of a winter-lit lake, and as cold.

It was the face of a strong-willed, even ruthless man — but not the face of a villain.

Greer was completely taken aback. 'It . . . it's not my imagination. He's — my husband — is taking him for a walk. They won't have gone far, in this rain . . . '

Her stumbling voice trailed off as the stranger shook his head at her. 'You told me on the phone that you didn't have a husband. Don't you remember? *Fortunately*, you said. Perhaps you'd like to revise that statement? They have their uses, like frightening people off, for instance.'

'You — you're Mr Meredith?' Greer managed to gasp. 'Then what do you imagine you're doing,' she bellowed, 'scaring me to death like that?' She didn't usually shout, but terror had given way to justifiable anger. She glared up at him, oblivious to the glistening drop of rainwater that still clung comically to the point of her nose.

'The very same. Byron Meredith at your service.' He made a bow, which Greer took to be mocking her and only served to increase her fury.

'What are you doing here? You do realise, don't you, that I thought you were a burglar, or worse? Can you imagine the effect that had on me, coming into what I'd supposed was an empty house, to hear footsteps upstairs?'

'If you recall, you demanded that I 'do something' about the state of the cottage. But now, when I obligingly drop everything else I was planning to do and come over to see what the trouble is, you complain and accuse me of trying to frighten you! It wasn't a deliberate act, I can assure you. I didn't know when you'd be back, so I let myself in. If I frightened you, then I apologise.'

He didn't look particularly repentant, leaning against the wall, his arms folded, taking up most of the room.

'And you do *have* the right to enter, when I'm not here?' she demanded.

His sigh was accompanied by a 'God give me strength' look. 'Now what are you accusing me of? Trespassing? I'm entitled to retain a key, I believe, and if I'm to put things right, what am I supposed to do? Make an appointment and come back when you're ready to receive visitors?' There was a gentle irony in his deep voice that stung her. He was making her appear a shrill, complaining shrew, though she had every justification for her complaints.

'Look, Mr Meredith, I'm paying good money to rent this dump, and all I can say is you must be making a fortune out of it. You obviously haven't spent anything on maintenance or cleaning for years, so now you're here, you may as well see what you can do about making the roof — and the front door — watertight.' She could feel spots of rain blowing through the gaps around the oak boards of the door, and suddenly realised just how wet she was, with her jeans dripping into her boots and water trickling down her neck from her saturated hair. Her new sweater hung misshapenly around her.

Of a sudden, perhaps due to delayed shock, she began to shiver, and her teeth chattered as she tried to speak. 'And wh-while you're a — about it, f-fix the f-floorboards.' She could hardly get the words out.

His eyes narrowed as he looked at her keenly. 'I'd better make it a priority to light the fire while you get out of those wet things. The back boiler heats the water, so you'd be able to have a bath in a hour or two.' He spoke as though it was the height of luxury and in the circumstances it probably was.

'In the meantime,' he continued, inspecting her mud-caked, high-heeled boots and soggy sweater, 'you'll catch your death if you don't get changed. I'd suggest you invest in a pair of wellies and a waterproof jacket if you intend spending a month here.'

'I doubt very much if I will.' She pushed past him to ascend the stairs. 'I'll get on to the letting agency and tell them that if they're calling this the perfect get-away-from-it-all, they're selling the idea under false pretences.' She squelched halfway up, then stopped and turned to him with her parting shot. 'I've had more aggravation in the past twenty-four hours than I've had all year.'

'Is that so? Then you must be a very spoiled young lady indeed,' he murmured to her back view as she disappeared with a toss of her head.

By the time she returned, her head wrapped in a towel, and dressed in her dusty-pink tracksuit, he had some logs spitting rather sulkily in the grate, and not the cheerful blaze she'd anticipated. 'Hm. Thought it would be a simple matter, once the logs had been located, to get a fire going,' she commented, maliciously, feeling disturbingly pleased to see the puzzled frown on his face. Spitefulness wasn't really a trait of her character, but she was still feeling very aggrieved, and he was the only target in her sights.

'There should be a good draught from this old chimney,' he muttered, but even as he spoke a great belch of dark, sooty smoke burst out of the chimney and filled the room with its acrid fumes.

Greer burst out laughing, for the first time seeing the funny side of all the minor disasters that had occurred since she'd arrived. 'Why I do believe the chimney needs sweeping! Like everything else here, it hasn't been attended to for years. Tell me, has anyone else stayed here, or has it been left to moulder away ever since Uncle Dai passed away twenty years ago?'

The effect of her words was electrifying. Byron spun round, his eyes blue ice. 'Can't you just stop being so clever for a while? Who do you think you are, anyway? Coming here, a stranger, and ordering me about? You, young lady, know nothing about me,' he prodded her in the shoulder, 'nor about living in the country, nor, it seems, about anything that's much use. You tell me it's not what you expected, or what you're used to; well let me tell you, *I* don't want *you* to stay here any longer. *I* don't want *you* in my cottage, not the other way around. You think you frighten me, threatening to report the state of the place to the agency? I don't give a damn. It was *they* who persuaded *me* to put the place on their books. Fell in love with it, they said,' he mimicked a genteel voice in a derisory manner. 'Roses round the door and honeysuckle under the windows! What nonsense! But, just like them, you've got this stupidly romantic notion of the countryside and you fold up completely over a little bit of rain.'

Greer was stunned by the ferocity of his attack, and leapt to her own defence. 'A little bit of rain? You must be joking! Look at it.' She gestured out of the clouded window set deep into the stone wall. 'It's a howling storm out there, and not much better in here.'

The choking smell of soot hung in the air and it covered the furniture in a fine layer.

'It's true that I've never lived in the country, but I came here to get away from — problems.' She wasn't about to tell this unsympathetic stranger any more than that. 'And what do I find? More problems, and I don't need all this.' She stamped her foot, then regretted it as he looked up from his crouched position at the fireside with an expression that spoke volumes.

He'd sized her up as a silly, spoiled

girl, and that was exactly how she was behaving. Inexplicable tears stung her eyes — it may have been the soot — and she turned away from him, hating him, hating the cottage, hating the awful, awful rain.

'I'll go and get my things. Perhaps you'd be so kind as to phone the company and make whatever arrangements are necessary for me to have a refund, because I certainly don't want to stay here, any more than you want me to.' His words still stung. She wasn't accustomed to rejection.

'What will you do?' He didn't sound as though he was particularly concerned.

'Drive to the nearest airport and catch a plane to the sun, I think. If I've any sense at all, that is. I should have done that in the first place.' It's for the best, she told herself, as she cleared her toiletries out of the tiny bathroom. She was still loath to admit defeat — it wasn't in her nature — but she'd never been made to feel less welcome in her life. Unused to being treated with such enormous unconcern, particularly by a member of the opposite sex, she felt unexpectedly hurt.

In different circumstances she might have found his total indifference a challenge, but she was cold, she was tired, and she was hungry. She needed more challenges in her life like a hole in the head, so the sooner she escaped, the better.

She looked uncertainly at her precious boots, a white watermark staining the dark leather. She'd ruined them, getting out of the car — the car! She'd forgotten it was firmly stuck in the mud, and if he went away and left her there . . .

'Mr Meredith,' she called, hurrying downstairs. 'Don't go just yet. I forgot to tell you — ' She stood in the living-room doorway, the towel falling onto her shoulders and releasing a cloud of blonde hair as she watched in astonishment while Byron poked around in the chimney with a broom handle.

His head had disappeared inside the fireplace and his long legs sprawled across the hearth. There was a muffled cry and he re-emerged, knocking his brow on the lintel in his hurry, just as a large, blackened bird's nest crashed down onto the smouldering logs. 'Thought as much,' he said to himself, unaware of her presence. 'Silly creatures, birds.' It seemed to Greer that his remark epitomised his attitude towards her, and, possibly, to womankind in general.

'Nearly as silly as women,' Greer couldn't resist the jibe, and he turned to look at her as he stood and brushed himself down. His eyes were thoughtful as he subjected her to a searching scrutiny, taking in the mass of unruly hair, and her slender-hipped shape in the easy tracksuit. She felt herself redden and damned him again for upsetting her normally cool composure.

'I don't think all women are silly

— not by any means. To be honest, I suppose I'm used to women who are practical, rather than merely — decorative. So perhaps I've been a bit hard on you, Miss — er.' He'd forgotten her name again, which showed just how much impact she'd made on him.

'Call me Greer,' she said, drily, thinking how far off the mark he was in his description of her as 'merely decorative'. If only he knew! But let him keep his illusions: after all, they'd never lay eyes on each other again, once he'd helped her get her car out of the mud.

'I hate to admit it, but I got my car well and truly wedged in some mud in the next field, and I need some help in getting it out.' May as well make the most of being regarded, for once, as a frail, stupid woman. 'I hate to trouble you, but do you think . . . ' Her voice trailed off as a devilish grin spread across his face.

'Been a disaster all round, hasn't it? The sooner you get back where you belong, amongst the jet-set or the yuppies or whatever, the better. You're obviously not cut out for rural living!'

'No, I've already come to that conclusion.' This time, it was *her* eyes that were glacial. 'So if you'll just lend me a hand, without all the comedy routine? Do you have a tractor, or something?'

'My old Land-Rover'll get you out, no problem. It's round the back, in the barn. It's like the house — leaks a bit — so I park it under cover.' He seemed remarkably cheerful for one so poverty-stricken, thought Greer, as she splashed after him across the yard. Heaven knows what kind of a state he lives in, if he thinks people will pay good money to rent this place, and as for his clothes . . .

They pulled in beside her car. 'You get in and steer while I tie a rope to her. Switch on the engine if it's got a steering-lock, but leave it out of gear and don't touch any of the pedals.'

'I'm not a complete bimbo,' Greer

snapped, and saw his shrug of indifference as he climbed into the Land-Rover.

It only took a minute — how easy when you had the proper vehicle — and they were back at the cottage with Byron untying the rope.

'Would you like a coffee before you go?' It seemed a little late in the day, but she might as well observe the proprieties.

He hesitated, and she assured him, with a grim little smile, 'You won't see me for dust once I've had a coffee and got my things together.'

He seemed relieved. 'Yes, I'll have a coffee.' And make sure I'm off the premises too, Greer finished for him, under her breath.

But as she boiled the kettle she could hear him banging away with hammer and nails, evidently having decided to execute at least some of the repairs. She hid a smile. She was used to people doing as she asked, but it was with something like a sense of triumph that she heard him bang the last nail in place before running lightly down the stairs.

He must have taken off his boots, she thought, and when, a minute or two later, she carried the coffee-cups into the lounge, she discovered he'd discarded the hooded jacket as well, and stood, hands behind his back in traditional masculine stance, before a roaring log fire.

'Must have been the bird's nest jamming the chimney that did it — coudn't draw up, you see.' He smiled, revealing square, evenly-shaped, gleaming teeth against his tanned face and dark beard. 'Makes a difference, doesn't it?'

Greer set the cups on a low table. It was plain in style, but made of a solid piece of mellowed walnut. All it needed was a little furniture polish and some loving care.

She looked around her.

Byron had switched on a lamp, which dispelled the gloom of the day, and the room, with its crammed bookshelves, deep chintz-covered sofa, and the water-colours of local views, took on an air of comfort.

'Are you sorry you're not staying, now?' Byron asked softly, seeing her expression.

'No, of course not.' Her response was a little too sharp. 'It looks better in here, but there are still holes in the roof, and it's just as dirty and damp elsewhere. I must have been mad to come here, when I could easily afford to go to one of the Greek islands, or Italy . . . somewhere warm, with plenty of nightlife. I was probably just feeling tired and jaded when I decided to spend a month in deepest Wales!' She shrugged, as though to dismiss her own lack of foresight.

'Must be hell,' he murmured, 'being jaded at living the high life. I daresay you needed to put some distance between yourself and all those attentive menfriends.' His full lips twisted in an ironic smile and, though it shouldn't have mattered at all, his attitude irked her. He wasn't too far from the truth, either.

He'd obviously prejudged her and found her wanting, even though he was clearly one of life's losers. She just wished he wasn't so disturbingly — male. She spent her working life surrounded by men of all ages, but thought of them as just 'people', apart from Steve, of course. But even he didn't cause her this strange feeling of unrest.

'You have a very stereotyped view of me,' she told him.

'I do?' The black eyebrows rose quizzically. 'I can only judge by appearances. A pretty blonde, not short of money, used to travelling around in her expensive car, and a life of idleness and self-indulgence, I'd say — '

'Then you'd say wrong.' She almost spat the words. 'If you always go by outward appearances, you must have a very narrow view of life.' She found herself wanting to tell him about herself, and how different she was from the impression he'd gained, but why bother?

'Oh, I've got it all wrong, have I?' He mimicked her London accent cruelly. 'I'd take some convincing of that. If anyone has tunnel vision, it's you. You thought you'd be wandering through cornfields picking wild flowers. How inconsiderate of the countryside to treat you to this deluge! And you couldn't switch on the central heating! Do you know — when you came back in here, I thought you'd actually be pleased to see a roaring log fire. I thought you'd curl up in front of it and we'd have a cup of coffee, and we might even, unlikely though it seems, have become friends.'

'Really? How cosy! And then, I suppose, you thought you'd curl up with me, and we'd be 'cosy' together, in front of the fire?' There was no mistaking the double entendre she implied.

Byron stared at her in contemptuous

silence. He obviously found the accusation so ridiculous as to be beneath his dignity to refute.

Why had she said such a thing? Greer felt herself grow hot with embarrassment as the silence grew. He'd made no attempt to flirt with her — far from it. He'd seemed unaware of her, physically.

Somehow she had to retrieve the situation, if only to salvage her own pride. 'I'm sorry,' she muttered. 'Forget I said that.'

'Forget?' he echoed. 'Forget I dropped everything to rush out here to carry out a few running repairs, tow your car out of the mud, get the fire going — and crack my head in the process — only to be accused of setting it all up for some kind of seduction scene?'

He threw back his leonine head and laughed scornfully, his strong white teeth gleaming in the leaping firelight, and if ever there were words she would have wished unsaid, she had just uttered them.

2

Moodily, Greer picked up her coffee and sipped the dark aromatic liquid. 'At least I've given you cause for amusement. Perhaps *I'll* see the funny side of things once I've left — which can't be soon enough as far as I'm concerned. I know, don't say anything' — she held out her hand as he looked about to speak ' — you'll be just as pleased to see the back of me. I didn't intend to accuse you of anything and I was wrong to say what I did. I'm sorry.'

Byron shrugged his wide shoulders. 'It's not important.'

'It is to me. I wouldn't want you to think — well, what you did. I suppose working in a man's world, you get used to fending off unwelcome propositions — you probably get over-defensive.'

'The secretary being chased around the desk by her boss syndrome?' Byron mused, and Greer didn't bother to appraise him of the fact that she was nobody's secretary — in fact, had a secretary of her own. 'Yes, I see what you mean. All I can say is, if you'd stayed here a month, I wouldn't have laid a finger on you! That's not to say you're not desirable, or that I don't have the normal reflexes of a healthy male animal.' Again his eyes studied her calmly, but more as he might assess a painting rather than a flesh and blood female. 'Let's just say I have other commitments.'

Of course! He was one of a dying breed, she thought. The faithful married man! She guessed him to be in his mid-thirties, a good ten years older than herself, and no doubt with a growing family to boot.

She blushed again at the thought of her unfair accusation, but at least there was one way she could make amends.

'Look, I've been very unfair about this. Obviously you need the rent, so don't worry about phoning Country

Idylls. You can use the money to carry out repairs. I can afford it — and you can probably do with it.'

It was instantly obvious that she'd said the wrong thing again. If she'd thought his eyes were cold before, now they glinted with the hardness of diamonds.

'You are, without a doubt, the most condescending female it's ever been my misfortune to encounter.' He was breathing hard, all traces of amusement gone, and began to stride up and down, visibly controlling himself. 'I wouldn't take a penny of your money! Daddy left it to you, no doubt, so it means nothing to you. You can scatter it about like some lady bountiful, and expect people to be grateful to you, to be humble in the face of such generosity — no, no, don't say another word . . . ' he shook his head fiercely as she tried to interrupt, to tell him how wrong he was about her, ' . . . I told you before, I don't want your wretched rent, and if I decide to spend any money on this place, or not, it's entirely my decision, and has nothing to do with you.'

Greer was appalled. What could she say — and why should it matter to her what he thought of her anyway?

The silence was filled only by the hissing of the logs and the constant drumming of the rain.

His furious pacing ceased as he stopped in front of her and she sat, her head bowed, wishing she'd never come here, never left her comfortable apartment, the security of her office, where she always said and did the right thing, to come here and be lectured by this man.

She stared at his be-socked feet, thinking, incongruously, how vulnerable they looked in their denim-blue socks, and wondering how she could find his feet so fetching when he was standing there castigating her.

'And there's another thing.' He hadn't finished with her yet. 'Before you make cute remarks about someone dying in a house, make sure of your facts first. It just might have happened.'

She watched his feet wheel away and cross the room.

He was leaving. She'd never see him again.

And it was beginning to dawn on her that she'd offended — no, hurt — him deeply, however unwittingly.

Nothing in her life had prepared her for this. She was out of her depth, afloat without a paddle.

Numbly, she heard him crashing about, putting on his boots, gathering his belongings, as she tried to think of what to say.

'Byron,' she called, but the only response was the thunder of the door as he slammed it behind him.

On her own, she looked round apprehensively. Had someone died in the cottage? She relished the thought of staying even less, though the fire was blazing merrily and the lamp shed a soft glow. She stood up. The sooner she was out of here, the better.

Aware that Byron was sitting in his

Land-Rover, stony-faced, waiting for her to leave, she carried her luggage out and climbed wearily into her car. She had no idea where she was going, only that she had to go.

Greer turned the ignition key. Nothing happened. Again she tried, but the engine refused to turn over. Again and again, in a panic now to be gone, but to no avail.

It was just too much. Greer, who couldn't remember having cried since she was a girl, felt tears of self-pity course down her cheeks, as though in sympathy with the relentless rain that streamed down the windows.

The sound of feet crunching on the gravel made her rub the backs of her hands across her face to brush away the evidence of her frailty.

Byron bent and opened the car door. His face was a caricature of patient resignation as he asked, 'What now?'

'It won't start. I can't believe it — it's never happened before.'

'And now you've flooded the engine.

You'll have to wait a while, give it time to dry out.' He hesitated, then she heard him sigh. 'You'd better wait in the house, where it's warmer.'

With a feeling of *déjà vu*, she followed him to the front door, where he stood aside for her to enter, though he still glowered unforgivingly.

Greer looked up and saw that his forehead was grazed where he'd hit it on the fireplace and instinctively she reached up to touch the small wound. 'You hurt yourself.'

'Don't pretend you care!' His response was ironic, and Greer went to push past him, but as she did so she saw his face, for the first time, in the full glare of daylight.

She gasped.

Although almost obscured by the dark beard and unruly hair, a deep scar ran down his face, traversing the tanned skin from close to his right eye to the point of his jaw. Though faded by wind and rain, the white line of scar tissue was wide and jagged.

Far from detracting from his attractiveness, it added a new, mysterious dimension to his rugged looks.

A question rose to her lips, but before she could voice it his eyes caught and held hers with ferocious intensity, as though he was forbidding her curiosity. Greer experienced a strange sensation, somewhere between fear and anticipation, almost as though she faced the intruder again, though this was an intruder of a very different sort.

This time it was her emotions and the well-guarded defences of her heart that were at risk. The sheer physical magnetism of this man who, until an hour or so previously, had been a complete stranger, threatened to assail her in a way she had never before experienced.

It was as though every cell in her body was aware of his nearness, every fibre of her being alerted to the peril of losing control over her own feelings.

A small shiver started at the base of her spine and travelled upwards, making her shake a little.

'You're cold.' It was as though he, too, though not actually touching her, could empathise with her slightest movement.

'Don't pretend *you* care,' she echoed his words, laughing shakily, and the bewildering moment of awareness passed.

In the vacuum it left, Byron hesitated, his eyes guarded again, and she regretted, fleetingly, that there'd be no opportunity to get to know him better. But they were worlds apart. Chalk and cheese. Town mouse and country rat!

Once she was on her way again, it would be as if he'd never existed as far as she was concerned, any more than he'd ever give her a second thought.

He was pulling up his hood to cover the abundant, near-black, unruly waves. 'Sorry your holiday was ruined, but as you say, you'll be more in your element in some foreign resort. You just don't fit in here. No offence intended, but you're a bit like a hot-house plant that's been stuck in the middle of a field! I'll ring the company and tell them to refund your money, though I suppose they'll want *their* pound of flesh.'

'I wish you wouldn't. Think about it — if I was a man, you wouldn't have reacted so angrily to my offering to waive a month's rent, would you? Because it wouldn't have hurt your masculine pride?'

She was removing her jacket and hanging it up so it could drip onto the flagstones, and as she turned back, ruffling her hair with her fingers, she found his eyes on the uptilt of her breasts.

There was a twist of wry amusement to his lips.

'It's a hypothetical situation I find hard to conjure up — you as a man. But I'll try. Hmm.' He held his chin in one hand, cupping his elbow in the other, and Greer knew he was mocking her, but held her tongue for once.

'You're probably right,' he conceded after a minute or two. 'If a man had offered to waive the rent, I'd have thought him an idiot and taken advantage. But something — call it old-fashioned gallantry if you want — prevents me from taking money from a woman.'

'But you will accept the rent — from me?' Once Greer had decided on a principle she stuck to it, against all odds.

He could be as stubborn as she. 'In all honesty, I can't charge rent to anyone, not the state the place is in. I've hardly set foot in it for . . . for two years.' For a fleeting moment a spasm of pain caused him to grimace, though Greer suspected the agony was mental, rather than physical, and was somehow connected with the cottage. 'You're not even going to stay here, so how can I take money from you, no matter what sex you are?'

Greer had met her match in the obstinacy stakes. 'OK. Have it your way.' At least she knew when she was beaten. 'But if Country Idylls insist on a percentage, at least let me pay that.'

Byron nodded, seemed to hesitate on the doorstep, then straightened his shoulders and stepped out into the lashing rain.

Greer stared after the tall figure splashing unconcernedly through muddy puddles, heedless of the splatter of raindrops from a broken gutter. A dozen questions crowded her mind, though she knew none would be answered. Once she'd got the car started, she'd drive to Heathrow and fly out to the sun. She'd lie mindlessly getting a tan and hope that her tangled emotions would unwind themselves eventually, and life would go on.

But in the meantime there were more mundane concerns. Like food. She suddenly realised she was starving hungry, and in no time at all she'd prepared herself a huge meal, following Byron's instructions on working the cooker, and consumed it in front of the friendly fire.

That over, she studied the contents of

the bookshelves, discovering Antonia Frazer's biography of Mary, Queen of Scots — something she'd always intended reading one day.

Contentedly, she settled herself on the sofa and began to read.

It wasn't until she realised that the light from one lamp was insufficient that she looked up and found it was growing dark, and the fire had burned low. Amazed, she looked at her watch, and found she'd spent the entire day reading.

Her book lay open, the fire glowed and, instead of leaving, she threw on some more logs, made herself a coffee, and with a sigh of sheer bliss returned to her book.

After all, she didn't *have* to leave.

Next morning she was awoken by the sound of noises on the roof. She put her head out of the window to find, to her delight, that the sun's rays were flooding the side of the mountain, burnishing the bronzed undergrowth with gold. Up above, in an unclouded sky, a white glider hung silently in the thermal currents before swooping sunwards and, even higher in the heavens, a plane had left its vapour-trail like white chalk against the celestial blue.

Large feet descended the ladder which leant against the wall and she looked up as blue overalls drew level, half expecting to see Byron. Instead, it was an elderly, ginger-haired man who looked at her in some astonishment.

'Didn't know there was anyone here — though I did wonder whose car it was,' he said conversationally as he passed. 'Fixing the roof for Mr Meredith, I am.'

'Great.' Greer beamed, at peace with the world. She hadn't given a thought to work, or Steven — or even ghosts — all night, though the near-silence had been a little unnerving for a city girl.

It wasn't until she heard a key turning in the lock, followed by firm footsteps, that she remembered her last waking thoughts. She'd wondered just what Byron Meredith would think of her if he really knew what she was like, and not the brainless, useless ornament he'd summed her up as?

But, she asked herself as she sipped her coffee, why should I care what he thinks?

The object of her thoughtful meanderings poked his head round the door. 'You didn't go!' His tone was accusatory.

'My car wouldn't start,' she lied, glibly. 'Must be something wrong with it — I'll get it seen to, don't worry.'

'And then you'll go?' He stood, hands on hips, wearing a faded check shirt with most of its buttons missing, revealing a sun-browned expanse of hairy chest. Greer couldn't stop herself comparing his physique with Steve's smooth, golden body. The men with whom she spent her working days were successful, and usually wealthy. They'd learned to regard the women in their lives as equals and had no need to assert a machismatic image. None of which applied to this man who now stood regarding her with something like alarm.

'I don't *have* to go,' she said, defensively. 'After all, I've still booked the cottage for a month, so I'm entitled to change my mind. I daresay you subscribe to the old saying that that's a woman's prerogative?'

It was the kind of thing a man like Byron would accept with an indulgent pat-her-on-the-head smile, she thought, wryly.

But he didn't. He sighed deeply.

'Women!' The expression was heartfelt.

'Yes, I'm afraid I am one. I must admit — I've never found it a handicap. But apparently you don't approve?' She stood and poured him a coffee. He looked as though he needed one.

Without glancing round, she knew he was observing the way her thin T-shirt clung to her uplifted breasts, and tucked neatly into her handspan waist. Her jeans were trim and well-fitting, over hips sleek as cat's fur.

'On the contrary, I definitely approve of women. Not all of them though — just the pretty ones.'

What a chauvinist, thought Greer, but smiled sweetly at him. May as well let him hang onto his illusions. He'd got her pigeon-holed as dumb but pretty, it might just be simpler to keep it that way! 'Pretty but not too bright?' she asked, smiling sweetly.

'Umm.' He stared at her over the rim of his cup and she saw that his lashes were long and dark, and his eyes even bluer on this sunlit morning.

Well, she thought, it might be fun, just for once, to pretend to be the dumb blonde he took her for. She swung her hair in a golden curtain and changed the subject. 'Now that the sun's shining, I don't find the countryside so uninviting. Will it be all right if I stay on here? I promise I won't complain about anything again.'

'Hm, that's a bit awkward.' He ran distracted fingers through his hair. 'I decided to get the place done up and put in good order so that . . . someone . . . could move in here.' Greer noticed his hesitation and the slight embarrassment.

'Permanently, or on a temporary basis?'

'That'll depend on her.' He was a man of few words when it suited him.

'I don't want to be bolshie, but I have paid a month's rent in advance.'

'But you said you were going — '

'And now I've said I'm staying.' Her features adopted a mulishness her employees would have recognised. 'I'm sorry, but you have to honour your contract with Country Idylls. And they have a contract with me.'

They glared at each other in mutual antagonism.

'Do you always get your own way?' he seethed at last.

'Always. So you may as well get used to it.'

'Do you know what I'd like to do? Put you over my knee and spank you! If you'd had that kind of treatment years ago you wouldn't act like a spoiled child.'

But Greer chose to ignore the gleam of amusement in his eyes. She didn't see any humour in such a remark. 'I wouldn't advise it. I'd sue for assault, as well as fraud, negligence and trespass,' she snapped.

'What have I done to deserve having this woman foisted on me?' Byron demanded of the ceiling, and then he wheeled on her. 'How about if I paid you your money back and you moved into a guest-house in the village? You wouldn't be so isolated, but you'd still have peace and quiet.'

He obviously wanted to be rid of her at all costs and, despite their lack of accord, that hurt. 'It looks like stalemate.' Greer lifted her chin and met his eyes squarely. 'You don't want me to stay, and I don't want to go.'

'And we're both as obstinate as each other.' He paused. 'I tell you what — I can have the outside done up, which shouldn't inconvenience you, and you can stay on, if that's what you really want.'

The sudden climb-down took her unawares. Greer studied him through narrowed eyes. 'Why,' she demanded, 'have you changed your mind?'

'It'd give you an opportunity to do a little soul-searching. It could even,' he grinned lazily, teasingly, 'make you become a better person!'

Greer gasped. If she'd ever been subjected to the badinage of an older brother she'd have known how to respond, but as it was she was stung to the quick by what she regarded as his criticism of her. Without thinking, her hand reached out to the mug and she picked it up and flung it straight at him. Byron ducked and the mug flew over his shoulder to hit the solid stone wall, smashing into a thousand pieces.

'You stupid little fool!' He grabbed her by the shoulders and shook her, his good-humour dispelled in an instant. 'When are you going to grow up?'

'I am grown up,' she yelled. 'I've built up my own business. I've got dozens of people working for me. I'm not just a dumb blonde, and I won't be treated like this. Let me go!' she screamed, as his grip tightened, and at that moment the face of the man on the ladder appeared at the window.

'Couldn't help hearing the rumpus.' He stared in amazement as Byron almost threw her back against the chair. 'Is everything all right?'

'Yes, Jack. Everything's fine. Just a slight difference of opinion.' The irony was heavy, his breathing hard.

'Thought I heard something breaking, and then all the shouting — '

'Yes, Jack, I — er — dropped something. Nothing to worry about. I'll be out to see you in a minute.'

The puzzled face withdrew and the silence between them was palpable.

'Don't you ever, ever, touch me again.' Greer's voice shook.

'Don't worry your pretty head, I've no intention of doing so. As far as I'm concerned, I haven't set foot here for two years and another month'll make no difference.'

'Good. Because I'll have you know I'm used to being treated with a degree of respect. I'm a successful business-woman in my own right — '

She wasn't prepared for his burst of cynical laughter. 'Successful? Maybe by your standards. So — you've made a bit of money, as you keep trying to remind me. That's not too difficult.' Her eyes flicked scornfully over his shabby attire, but he ignored her raised eyebrows. 'You're a tough, shrewd businesswoman? Congratulations! I hope it keeps you warm in bed!'

And with that parting shot he spun on his heels and was gone, with a banging of doors that was becoming familiar.

Greer sat, staring at the debris. She'd never allowed herself to be provoked into such an act before. In fact she prided herself on her cool control. What was it about this infuriating man that had driven her to behave so badly?

3

It was some time before she managed to calm herself sufficiently to decide what to do with the day that stretched blissfully before her. No deadlines to meet, no meetings to attend, no staffing problems!

From now on, she'd devote herself to herself. No doubt a certain someone would find that selfish and egotistical, but that was his problem.

She set out for a long, contemplative walk. It was Steve she was here to think about; Steve, who'd been part of her life for nearly four years. Steve, who loved her, knew the way her mind worked, and respected her.

Greer walked for miles, clambering breathlessly up the hillsides, until she paused and looked back at the mosaic of fields and woods.

Houses grown tiny by distance were

scattered in the lush valley, and the ruined tower of a border castle was outlined dramatically against the far skyline. It was a long while since she'd been so utterly alone, and it was what she needed.

Even so, the long shadows of late afternoon found her hurrying back towards the cottage and thinking that perhaps, after all, a little human company wouldn't go amiss. She could go out for a meal — no rule that said she had to spend the month like a cloistered nun. It might be fun to discover a good eating-place that she could tell her friends about.

She hadn't come to any decision about Steven, but a day without the stresses of work had been calming — once Byron had cleared out of her life.

A short-lived acquaintance, and one she could have done without altogether!

She hummed as she tucked her white silk shirt into black cords, and clinched her waist with a heavily buckled belt; then, swinging her glove-soft scarlet leather jacket over her shoulders, she ran lightly downstairs and out into the mild night air. The total darkness of the countryside, the deep silence, were strange to her, as were the expanse of starlit sky, the clarity of the clean air. She took a gulping breath of it and decided this holiday was, after all, exactly what she needed.

It was the lights that drew her to the long low building. Glowing incandescently, a little misted at the edges, like tiny beacons. She pulled into the forecourt and noted the name on the floodlit sign. 'The Swan'.

The saloon bar was comfortably full and she glanced around for somewhere to sit, aware that she was the focus of many eyes. After all, she was a stranger in these parts, and there weren't too many of those. There was nothing for it but a stool at the bar, as all the tables seemed occupied, but no sooner had she seated herself and ordered a Perrier water than a young man perched on the empty stool beside her.

Studiously avoiding even glancing in his direction, she called for the menu and was surprised at the contents. She'd been expecting something fairly run-of-the-mill, but there was a wide choice of unusual dishes and it was some time before she beckoned the waiter to place her order.

'Whose party are you with, madam?' he asked, pencil poised.

'I'm on my own,' she said, surprised.

'You haven't booked? Oh, I'm sorry, we don't have a table free — '

'You can share mine,' the fresh-faced young man seated beside her broke in eagerly. 'It looks as though I've been stood up, so — '

Greer was already shaking her head when another voice broke into the confusion. 'No problem. The lady's with me. Go ahead and order, Greer.'

She looked up at the brilliantly lit mirror behind the bar, to see Byron standing behind her, head and shoulders above her and her unwelcome companion.

She whirled round. 'Thanks, but no thanks.' Her eyes widened as she became aware of the change in him. The tousled hair had been tamed into submission and lay neatly, if a little long, close to his head. The hooded jacket had been replaced by a sweater that had the unmistakable softness of cashmere, and his jeans by impeccably tailored slacks.

By the time she reached the shoes, which had the soft gleam of expensive leather, she was beginning to wonder if she was dreaming. These immaculate, expensive clothes had never seen a speck of mud, and the trousers must have been specially made for his long legs and narrow hips.

What had happened to the poverty-stricken farmer?

'Now that you've finished your tour of inspection, would you like to retract that refusal?' She met his eyes, the reflected lights adding a new dimension to the deep, dark blue, warming them, and he was actually smiling!

For a moment she was tempted, then remembered how insufferable he'd been that very morning, and how he'd humiliated her.

'No. I'm particular about my dining companions.'

He lowered himself onto the vacant stool, the importunate young man having disappeared rather rapidly. 'Let me see.' He thrust out his wrist, pushing back the beige cashmere to reveal his watch. A heavy, gold Omega, Greer noted, and not the steel waterproof he'd worn that morning. 'It's just after nine. By the time you've driven over there, you might just get a Chinese take-away in Hereford. Otherwise, you might as well go back to the cottage and eat bread and cheese.'

He folded his arms and stared at her imperturbably.

He was disturbingly close to her, his knees brushing her leg, his cologne, heady but not overpowering, reinforcing this disturbing new image of him — an image that had unbalanced her altogether.

'What were you going to order?' His voice was low, almost gentle, and lured her into his trap.

'I *was* going to have Crevette Rosé and medallions of venison — ' she began, and before she had time to protest he was clicking his fingers to summon the waiter.

'Crevette Rosé and the venison for the lady, and smoked trout and rack of lamb — underdone — for me, please, Javier. Oh, and a bottle of Pinot to start with.'

'My God, you just presume too much.' Greer tried to get to her feet, to walk out, even if it was to bread and cheese. 'Didn't you hear me, I said NO, N-O! I want to have a pleasant evening on my own — is it too difficult for you to appreciate that I couldn't tolerate your undivided attention all evening?'

His hand detained her, encircling her

wrist with its powerful grip. 'Who said it was my undivided attention? What makes you think I'm alone?'

Of course, he must be with his wife. She glanced around, wondering where she could be. 'You're with your wife?'

His dark eyebrows rose and he gave another of his rare smiles. 'No, I was having a drink with a client, but I'm not sure if he intends to stay for a meal. Will you excuse me for a moment while I ask him?' He released her wrist and slid his hands around her waist, lifting her effortlessly back onto the stool. 'You're looking very beautiful tonight,' he murmured, unexpectedly, and then left her, bemused and bewildered, while he strode across the bar to talk with a craggy, elderly man in a tweed suit.

Why am I allowing myself to be taken over by this man, Greer wondered, but knew that part of her was intrigued by the transformation. Just who — and what — was he, this Byron Meredith?

'No, he said he wouldn't impose himself on us,' Byron said with a twitch of the lips as he returned. 'Thought he'd leave the field clear for me.'

'The only reason I'm joining you is that there isn't another table.' Greer was aware that she sounded bad-tempered and ungracious, but she really didn't care. If this man insisted on foisting himself on her, that was his lookout. He seemed oblivious to her ill-humour, however, and intent on being as charming as he knew how.

'Come and sit down at the table, and let's pretend we're friends.' His grasp was warm and firm and they walked into the restaurant hand-in-hand, which Greer found disconcerting.

'Won't people think it strange?' she asked. 'I mean — won't your wife wonder . . . I should imagine in an area like this, word would soon get back to her, that you were seen dining with a woman . . . ' Her voice trailed away.

'My wife? You do seem overly concerned — that's the second time you've brought up the subject in the last ten minutes. Don't you think that's something for me to worry about, not you?'

She shrugged. So be it. As he said, it wasn't her problem if he got himself talked about.

The restaurant was a converted barn, with an elaborate arrangement of ancient oak beams supporting its high ceiling, and an uneven brick floor that Greer, looking at it from her professional viewpoint, was sure must present dire problems for the waiting-staff.

It was furnished with an assortment of antique tables and chairs, giving it the ambience of a home, rather than a restaurant; but the clientele were dressed to kill and Greer suspected she'd stumbled upon the classiest establishment in the vicinity.

So what was Byron, the poor farmer, doing here — though not the slightest bit out of place, indeed, the most striking-looking man there, with his piratical beard and scar contrasting dramatically with the understated, softly muted outfit he wore.

She frowned across at him, determined not to be charmed. 'I don't understand. I mean, I don't want to be rude,' she ignored the way he raised his eyebrows disbelievingly at that, 'but this morning, and yesterday, you looked as though you hadn't got two halfpennies to rub together. And now you're looking extremely prosperous, to say the least.'

'Ah, I thought I detected a subtle change in your attitude. Still hostile, but a mite less disparaging, I do believe.' The charm had been switched off like a tap. His jaw-line, never less than determined, was steely.

'*I'm* hostile? If I am, it can only be because of the way you speak to me and treat me! You seem incapable of extending normal courtesy and civility for more than a few minutes at a time. Of course I'm impressed. It's only natural, isn't it, to admire success and to pity failure? *I* know how hard it is to achieve success, believe me.'

'Oh yes, you were telling me, weren't

you, how you weren't a spoiled child — how wrong I was about you?' His expression was bland, as though the scene in the kitchen had been an ordinary conversation. 'So tell me, what do you do that keeps you in such style? Am I to assume that 'Daddy' doesn't pay for everything, then?'

'I don't even have a 'Daddy',' she flashed, her eyes stormy. 'I've had to stand on my own two feet ever since I can remember. I'm one of those well-known statistics, a single child of a single-parent family. That teaches you how to deal with life like nothing else.'

She tried to keep the bitterness from her voice, but some of the anguish of her early childhood rushed back.

'My mother had to work to support us, and became a buyer in one of the big London stores, which meant she never got home before sixish, and worked on Saturday mornings as well.'

She took a sip of the wine, golden as corn, and Byron waited, silently, for her to continue.

'I seemed to spend the whole of my childhood wrestling with my homework, alone, in a drab rented flat. She had to work behind a bar on some evenings as well, to make ends meet. That's the background I came from, you see.' She wondered why she'd unburdened herself to Byron. Hardly anyone, even Steve, knew about her early days, before she'd achieved money and success.

'So that's why you went so over the top about the cottage being cold and damp — it probably triggered off some memories of the past.'

'I'm not that self-analytical, but you could be right.' She took another sip of the heady, aromatic wine, whose bold taste conjured up sun-bathed Italian hillsides. 'Um, this is lovely.'

'Don't change the subject. I want to know all about you.'

'Why?'

Her chin held high, she gazed back at him challengingly.

'Because,' in a voice soft as honey,

'I'm beginning to think you're a rather special person.'

The candle between them flickered and his eyes were lambent pools.

'I'm no more special than the next person who decided to rise above their beginnings. There are plenty of us. It just takes single-minded determination — and it helps if you're a workaholic, like me.' She tried to be dismissive but he wasn't letting her off the hook that easily.

'So what do you do?'

'I've got my own catering business.' She shrugged, and moved aside to allow the waiter to place a bowl of translucently pink prawns on a bed of crushed ice before her.

'It is our own special mayonnaise,' he told her, placing a dish of thick, creamy sauce the colour of buttercups almost reverently beside her.

With pleasurable anticipation, Greer delicately peeled a giant-sized prawn, revealing its succulent pink-tinged flesh, which she then plunged into the fragrant sauce.

She was aware that Byron was watching her every movement.

'From that, I gather that you don't do the cooking yourself.' At her continued silence he pressed his questioning. 'You're certainly not my idea of an apple-cheeked, floury-handed cook!'

'No.' Greer smiled at the picture he conjured up. 'Though I used to, when I first started. Had to — I was a one-woman band, then. My first job was cooking for a friend's party, and it kind of mushroomed from that. After a few months I seemed to be cooking all the time . . . parties, private dinners . . . nearly every night of the week, and always at weekends. I started taking on assistants, then I bought a van and had the name of the business painted on it.'

She stopped, remembering how proud she'd been. 'I'll never forget that day — and now we have ten vans, all pale grey with my matt-black logo on them. I've over thirty employees and we've just moved into smart new offices off the Bayswater Road.'

'So why are you here?'

The abrupt question took her unawares. 'I told you. To get away from all the hassle.'

'But you love it! You said — you're a workaholic. Workaholics don't bury themselves in the country for a month. What are you running away from?'

'I'm not running away — ' She stopped, to give herself time to gather her thoughts, squeezing the lemon from her finger-bowl. 'At least, not from the business. There's someone — '

'Ah. Do I detect some love-interest in the story?' Byron's deep voice sounded only mildly curious, yet she felt a tension in the air as he waited for her reply.

She nodded, trying to picture Steve, and yet somehow not being able to do so. She could only focus on the darkly bearded face so close to her own, the leaping firelight from the nearby blazing logs revealing the strange scar that seemed to go so much deeper than a mere surface injury.

'I'm trying to decide,' she said eventually, her voice husky, 'what to do about him.'

'He's asked you to marry him?' He reached forward and wrapped his fingers around hers, his thumb linking with her thumb in a heart-thumpingly intimate manner. 'Why is it such a difficult decision? Do you love him?'

'I — I thought I did . . . but I'm not absolutely certain. He wants me to take him into the company, as well.'

She was only too aware that Byron still held her hand, his thumb idly stroking hers.

'Sounds as ambitious as you are. Is it you he wants, or the business?'

'What kind of a crack is that?' She was immediately on the defensive.

'Well, why should you take him into the company, when you're the one who built it up? You have to be careful, Greer — it's a jungle out there.'

She snatched her hand away. 'And what do you know about it? I can look after myself, you know. Like I said, I've done so ever since I can remember. Steve's already more or less in the business. He's been my accountant for some years, and when I needed some more capital, about a couple of years ago, he offered to put it up himself. Now he wants to come into it full-time.'

'Rather than just a sleeping partner?' Byron gibed, but she chose to ignore the innuendo.

'It's become very time and energy consuming, and I think it will probably be a good idea.'

'You don't sound too sure.'

'I'm used to being on my own.'

'And you can't give even a little bit of yourself, can you? You've been driven all these years by the spectre of your mother and your lonely childhood, so you *had* to make a success of your life, didn't you? And now you don't want to endanger all you've achieved. You have to let a little love in as well, believe me.'

'You're an expert on the subject, are you?' Her blue eyes flashed.

'I know what it's like to face life without it.' His mouth tightened and she knew he had no intention of being as self-revelatory as she had. In any case, he was saved from elaborating on the subject by the arrival of their main course.

'I didn't know it would be so civilised. I can't fault the food at all, even though I *am* a professional,' she said, biting into delicious al dente fresh vegetables.

'We're not totally uncivilised — we may be Celts, but we do appreciate the finer things in life.' There was an edge of amusement in Byron's voice, though Greer was relieved the conversation had taken a lighter tone.

'Like wine, women and song?' Her mouth curved upwards in a slightly mocking smile.

'I'm certainly fond of wine and, being Welsh, singing's as natural as breathing. As for women, well, yes, I suppose you could say I do appreciate them.'

'En masse, or one at a time?' she

asked, demurely, and he threw back his head and chuckled, revealing his strong, gleaming teeth.

'I'm beginning to see how I underestimated you,' he said, his flagrantly blue eyes studying her with even greater interest. 'I have to admit, I had you down as a stupid, spoiled girl who'd got herself into a situation she couldn't handle, but now I realise you had good reasons for coming here, and you've got the determination to see it through.' His hand covered hers as it lay on the table, but it was more a sympathetic gesture than a romantic one. The mere friendly pressure of his warm palm evoked a response of such physical power that she trembled to think what a kiss might do to her, though why such a thought should enter her head she had no idea.

This is crazy, she thought. I love Steven, so behave.

But the tumultuous stirrings inside herself told her otherwise.

'You must take care, you know,' he was saying, gently. 'The trouble with being successful is that there's always someone wanting to step into your shoes, to stab you in the back. I don't know why I should care, but I do, and I wouldn't want it to happen to you. Are you quite sure it's you Steve wants, and not control of the business?'

'You think that's impossible, I suppose? Someone wanting me? Well, of course he does — he loves me deeply, and it's absolute nonsense to suggest he has any ulterior motive. And what would you know about success, anyway? You've put a good face on things this evening, presumably to impress somebody or other, but the reality of the situation is that you're one of life's losers, Byron, and it seems to me you're pretty bitter and twisted about it, otherwise you wouldn't cast such aspersions on others.'

Her angry flow of rhetoric, which had been increasing in volume, was interrupted by the arrival of the restauranteur, asking discreetly if everything was to their satisfaction.

'By the way,' the man turned to Bryon, having received their assurances that the food (if not the company, thought Greer) was up to standard, 'how's the horse? The one that fell last weekend. No lasting damage, I hope?'

'No, he's fine. Be racing again soon, though I shouldn't put any money on him — he can't seem to stay upright all the way round.'

'You have racehorses?' Greer interrupted, taken by surprise.

There was astonishment on the face of the proprietor. 'Well, of course he has racehorses. How could he train them otherwise?' He talked as though to a simpleton and Greer flushed. 'He's well known as a trainer, madam. In fact, I'd assumed you were one of his owners.' The poor man was looking highly embarrassed but Greer was too angry to worry about that.

'No, I don't have *that* kind of money.' Somewhere in the recesses of her mind a bell rang. Byron Meredith. Yes, she had heard the name. Which meant he was far from being a poverty-stricken family man — one of life's losers, in fact. Her cheeks burned. And *she'd* offered *him* money!

That he chose to look little better than a tramp at times, that the cottage was in its present state, wasn't because he hadn't the money. He had, quite deliberately, it seemed, made her look a complete and utter fool, not disabusing her of her misconceptions.

She pushed back her chair and stood.

'Where are you going?' He looked up sharply, taking in her high colour and mutinous expression.

'I'm not sitting making polite conversation any more! You, with your leaking car and your shabby clothes,' she hissed, 'making remarks about me being a hot-house flower, when you must mix with far wealthier people than I could ever hope to be, if you train their horses. But I doubt you're allowed the luxury of being rude to them, or they'd take their business elsewhere. Well, you've made me look a fool, and I hope you're satisfied! Let me know how much the bill comes to and I'll pay my half. After all, I only sat with you because there wasn't anywhere else.' And she rushed from the restaurant before the hot, stupid tears began to fall.

4

'Leave me alone, leave me alone.' Greer's own cries woke her in the deep dark of the night. For seconds she experienced the terror of a lost child, not knowing who, or where, she was.

Then, she realised, she was Greer Jameson, successful career woman, alone, in Ty Bach, in the heart of Wales.

Alone.

No need to implore anyone to leave her alone. Steve had been quite happy to let her go. 'Don't you worry,' he'd said, 'I can run things just as well as you can. You've got to learn to delegate management.'

Greer sat up in bed. Of course she could trust Steve. Byron had been mischief-making, trying to implant a tiny seed of doubt in her mind. She hugged her knees, and watched the first glimmer of dawn faintly outlining the deep-set window as she thought back to the beginnings of her relationship with Steve.

At first, they'd lunched together occasionally, purely in the course of business, and a mutual respect for each other's abilities had grown into an after-hours friendship.

Greer tried to remember when it had begun to be something more than just friendship. She'd never experienced any clamorous responses to his kisses; they were reassuring, comforting. She looked forward to seeing him, to their outings to the theatre, or to see the latest film everyone was raving about, but not with a thunderous beating of her heart at meeting her lover.

She shivered in the cool night air and huddled under the blankets again, waiting for sleep to enfold her. But when it did, it brought with it dreams this time, and not nightmares. And in her dreams she was carried away on a tide of passion by a tall stranger with a cruelly scarred face, eyes of brilliant blue and a dashing black beard.

Days passed in walking and thinking and it was with some surprise that she realised late one evening there was someone banging on the door. The only people she'd seen all week had been the builders, arriving as she was setting out, and leaving as she returned with a ferocious appetite and a satisfactory weariness of body and soul. 'Who is it?' She was, after all, alone.

'Byron.'

She felt oddly short of breath as she opened the door and looked at him as coolly as she knew how. 'Sorry, were you just going to bed?' he asked, taking in her attire of periwinkle-blue bathrobe and mules.

'Yes. Did you want something?' Coolly. Not inviting him in.

'I brought round that bill. You were serious, weren't you — about paying your half? I'm not bothered, but knowing what prickly pride you have, I thought you might be offended if I didn't give you the opportunity. I'd have come sooner but I've been at the races all week.'

'With any success?' asked Greer, offhandedly.

'Some. Couple of winners and others placed. You'll catch your death standing on the doorstep. Are you going to invite me in, or am I strictly *persona non grata?*'

Reluctantly, Greer stood aside.

'You've got the fire going,' he said, unnecessarily, as the bright flames danced in the draught.

'Yes, I'm surviving.'

'You certainly are.' He looked round the room, at the furniture gleaming with beeswax, the voluptuous pink and white blossoms of the gloxinia plants on the window-sill, the bowl heaped with fruit. 'It looks just like it used to when . . . ' he hesitated, clearing his throat huskily, 'when I used to visit here.' He turned and kicked a log into place, making it crackle. 'What have you been doing all week?' he asked, changing the subject. 'Have you been bored?'

'Heavens no! I've been getting myself fit. I saw some pony-trekkers up on the mountains the other day and I thought I might like to do that. Do you know where they're based? I could go riding tomorrow.'

'Have you ever done any riding?' He looked at her doubtfully.

'A bit. Not much, I'm afraid, and it was years ago,' she admitted.

Byron was thoughtful, standing with his back to the fire, looking down at her, at her long slender legs gleaming and smooth, the play of firelight on her golden hair, and the faint flush of her cheeks from so much fresh air. 'I'll call for you in the morning with a couple of horses,' he said, finally. 'Could do with a gallop myself.'

She was startled. 'I didn't mean — '

'No, I know you didn't, and I know you don't enjoy my company. But those nags they have at the stables aren't what you might call an exciting ride — and we both know how much you like a challenge.' He was mocking her again.

'Yes, I do.' She was going to give as good as she got from now on. 'But I'm not suicidal either. I'm not riding one of your racehorses.'

'And I wouldn't entrust one of them to a novice rider — they're much too precious. No, I've got my own horse, and another that belongs to my mother, except she hardly rides any more. The poor old thing could do with some exercise — the horse, not my mother. What do you say?'

'At the risk of repeating myself, won't your wife mind you gallivanting over the mountains all day with a strange female?'

He bent down, placing a hand on each arm of the chair, leaning towards her, his cologne familiar yet disturbing. 'As it obviously causes you so much concern, I have to tell you. I don't have a wife — I have never had a wife, in fact, so how about it? Is it a date, tomorrow at nine?'

But the next morning Greer stepped back, aghast, as the sound of frantic legs kicking out in all directions from the rear of the horse-box that Byron had driven up in. 'I can't ride that!' she cried, but all Byron did was stand, hands on hips, and grin diabolically.

'He'll calm down, once we get him out. Not used to the box, you see. He never gets the chance for an outing, and he's a bit long in the tooth to learn new tricks.'

He opened the side door of the box and, making soothing noises all the while, untied the halter. With infinite patience, he gently backed the nervous animal down the straw-strewn ramp.

'There we are, old feller. Safely back on *terra firma* again.'

His hands, so strong and capable, were tender as they stroked the horse's neck, and, though the whites of his eyes still showed his alarm, the horse did appear to be happier now that he was out of the horse-box. However, Greer's alarm did *not* abate.

'Here, grab hold of these,' Byron threw her the reins, 'and walk him round quietly while I get Forester out. It's all right — he won't bite, or bolt! You have *seen* a horse before, haven't you?' He was enjoying himself hugely at her expense.

'Yes, but he's a bit big, and I haven't seen one at such close quarters, not for years anyway. I'd forgotten how overpowering they can be.' Gingerly, she took the reins and made an encouraging noise with her tongue.

'Just tell him to walk on,' Byron instructed, and when she spoke softly to the horse she found, to her relief, that he walked quietly beside her up the drive and round the side of the house.

'There's a good boy,' she said, still tense, but enjoying the sensation of leading him along and seeing his terror abate.

By the time they rounded the other corner Byron had the big bay stallion out of the box and was tying him up to the gate-post. 'I'll get Forester tacked up first, while you get to know Barney, then I'll give you a hand with him.'

'Right,' she agreed, hoping he'd do more than give a hand, as she hadn't a clue how to 'tack up' and was sure the horse would sense this.

'Walk on, Barney,' she said, and the grey looked at her out of the corner of his eye before obeying, as though to say, who is this strange creature? Greer stroked his harsh mane, and he moved off again, appearing to accept her authority.

A few more quick turns around the cottage and she was beginning to feel a warm, unspoken companionship with Barney, as his neatly shod feet clicked importantly along.

'I'm going to enjoy riding you, pal,' she confided, and realised that Byron had intended that not only should she win Barney's confidence, but that her own should be bolstered as well.

'Right you are, bring him here. He laps up all the fuss and attention — he's more like a woman, but then they usually are, these geldings.'

Greer hid a smile at Byron's words. He was clearly in his element with the horses.

'Take this,' he handed her a well-polished saddle, 'and put it on his back. Then he knows what he's in for!'

The horse gave a little nicker of apparent pleasure as she heaved the saddle over his broad back and he stood still whilst Byron initiated her into the mysteries of bits and bridles and reins and girth-straps.

Byron stood behind her, his arms reaching round to assist with stubborn buckles or to show her where one of the many straps went, and though the horse was placid, Greer was anything but.

The feel of Byron's muscular chest moving against her back, the light embrace of his strong arms, sent her pulses racing. He was so close she was sure he must hear her heart pounding as her very nerve-ends tingled with awareness.

'Um, do you always smell so good?'

Not until the horse was ready did he turn his attention to her, and then he wrapped his arms around her shoulders oh-so-lightly.

'We city girls never forget our perfume,' she told him, leaning back slightly, enjoying the unfamiliar sensation of security that his stance gave her. 'And today I need it to cover up the smell of fear.' She was only half joking.

'You're not frightened now?' His grip on her tightened so that the whole length of her body rested against his and she let her head fall back onto his broad shoulder. His beard brushed her forehead.

'Not of the horse. Not any more.'

'Of what then? I didn't think anything scared you, so what's the problem?'

'I rather think *you* are.' The words were out before she could retrieve them and she felt him tense; then he gripped her shoulders and turned her to face him. 'I came down here to work out my priorities, and I can't seem to work up any enthusiasm for the ones I thought were important.'

'Because of me?' His eyes were like lasers, burning into her head.

'Oh, Byron, don't interrogate me. I'm so confused, I'll just say something silly, which I'll regret later, and you'll think me a fool again.'

'No — I think you've lived that down. In fact, you've shattered my misconceptions. Perhaps brains and beauty can go together after all!'

His tone was lightly teasing and she was grateful to him for relieving the tension before she admitted that the only truth she'd learned was that she could never live with Steve. Because she knew now she'd never been in love with him.

Barney impatiently scraped the ground and she broke away, before Byron could kiss her, which for some crazy reason she was sure he'd been about to do, and before she could respond, as she knew she would, with an ardour that would have betrayed her.

'Let's get this show on the road, then,' she said brightly, if a little shakily, and gathered up the reins.

'Tighten up his girth first,' Bryon's voice was oddly hoarse, 'and up you get.' She put her foot in the stirrup and he helped her swing up. 'You shouldn't wear jeans for riding, you know. Those heavy seams could make the insides of your thighs red raw.'

'So — I'll buy some jodhpurs tomorrow,' she said, primly, 'and the only person to suffer if I have sore thighs will be me.'

After a few words of instruction she settled into the rhythm of the good-natured horse and was even able to keep her seat when, following Byron's lead, she told Barney to 'trot on' up the road leading to the common.

The day was clear and bright, the skies washed a pale, cloud-strewn blue like a streaky water-colour painting, the green of the mountains harsh in its intensity, with the grey bareness of their upper heights a little forbidding.

'Just the day to clear away the cobwebs,' Byron called from his superior position mounted on his magnificent stallion. 'And I must say, you seem to be getting the best out of poor old Barney.'

'We've got a good thing going between us, haven't we, old love?' Greer patted his smooth sturdy neck and his ears twitched in response.

'Hm, I think you're trying to make me jealous. I might have a chance competing with Steve, but Barney — with his mournful brown eyes and unquestioning obedience? Not an earthly. Come on, though, we've got a lot of ground to cover if we're to make it over the mountain for lunch.'

'Over the mountain?' Greer gasped. 'You expect me to ride over that on my first day out?'

'Well, strictly speaking, it's over a gap in the mountain so you'll be all right. You've taken to it like a duck to water, and a hot bath'll take away all the aches and pains.'

After a hard morning's ride they reached the crest and looked down on a cluster of grey stone buildings and a ribbon of road which followed the course of a swiftly flowing stream.

'Not far now,' he called and, without pausing to admire the breathtaking view of the wooded valley, was off down the slope on his sure-footed beast.

'Time and Byron wait for no man,' Greer muttered to herself, and halted her horse rebelliously, waiting for Byron to notice their absence.

'What's wrong?' he called, reappearing a few moments later.

'What's your hurry? Can't we stop for a rest?' Greer pleaded. He'd been right about the inappropriateness of jeans, as she was already painfully aware.

'I was going to stop at the Cwm Inn for lunch, but if you want a break now, follow me. There's a clearing just down here.'

Having tied up the horses, Greer sank gratefully to the ground, stretching full-length on the mossy turf. The sun on her eyelids was deliciously warm as, with a happy sigh, she tucked her hands behind her neck and relaxed.

She felt Byron lie down beside her and, when she cautiously opened one eye, found he was propped on one elbow, watching her. 'Sorry, was I driving you too hard?'

'I'm not as fit as you are — and it's turned quite hot, hasn't it?'

'Feel free to strip off, if you wish. Don't mind me — I'm harmless!'

At that her eyes opened wide. 'That I find hard to believe!' She laughed, and, squinting against the shafts of sunlight, looked up at the dark outline of his head.

He was so close to her and the sunshine so dazzling she felt oddly dizzy. 'Oh, Byron,' she murmured, 'I don't want you to be harmless. I feel like living dangerously,' — and to hell with his 'commitment', whatever it might be. He wasn't married, that much he'd told her, so . . . all's fair in love and war. I want him, and I'm used to getting what I want, so I'm going to have this wonderful, enigmatic man, just for a while at least.

'Is that a challenge?' he murmured, in a voice that was dangerously, thrillingly, low. 'Because, if so, I should warn you — there's nothing I enjoy better than bringing a wild filly under my control.'

'I'm not one of your horses.' She reached out a hand and touched his beard. It looked so dark and dense she expected it to feel harsh against her fingertips, but it was soft and vibrant and she found her fingers drifting through its springiness.

'And I'm not one of your puppets. I won't jump when you give the orders. You know that, don't you?'

Greer frowned. Her fingers ceased their caressing movements. 'I'm not giving orders, am I?'

'Not in so many words, no. But you're not afraid to let me know that you want me, and I'm not accustomed to that, I have to admit. The way you're lying there, inviting me . . . hell, it'd take a stronger man than I am to resist you,' he ended on a groan.

'Then don't resist,' Greer urged him, shamelessly. She'd never before desired a man as she now desired him and she was so used to taking the initiative she had no inkling how much her boldness took his breath away.

'Greer,' he moaned, the Welsh lilt in his deep voice giving her name a unique intimacy which sent a quiver through her. 'You know I want you. I've been wanting you every damn moment I've been with you — '

'You have?' She lifted her head to stare at him. 'You seemed so indifferent to me — '

'Indifferent — if only you knew! But a man can only take so much — '

The bright sunlight was blotted out as he leant over her and she felt his warm breath on her face. Her heart skipped a beat and a small pulse in her throat began to throb.

She was on shifting sands, totally out of control for once, as though a woman possessed, overtaken by a longing that was primaeval in its unthinking urgency.

She opened her eyes to find that his face was only inches from her own, his eyes glowing in the reflected light, his wide firm lips slightly parted as they descended, deliciously slowly, to hers.

Their lips moulded together in perfect unison in a rhythm of undulating softness and fiercer, hungry passion. It was the first, experimental kiss of lovers, yet to Greer it was familiar . . . the kiss she'd been awaiting half her life. It was like awakening after a long, dreamless sleep.

His kiss deepened, commanding her response, and she opened her mouth in abandoned sensuality, accepting him, giving herself to him joyfully. She wrapped her arms around him, lifting herself from the ground so his arms could encircle her, and they lay on the sun-dappled earth, lost to the world in an embrace so fierce it was as though they wished to dissolve into each other.

At last they both gasped for breath.

'Oh, my darling, my beautiful, wonderful Greer.' Byron's lips were everywhere, kissing the salty skin of her brow, tugging her earlobes, nuzzling erotically in the curve of her neck, delicately nipping the tip of her nose, before returning, feverishly, to her mouth.

He released her a little, took some of his weight on an elbow, and with his free hand pushed up the fine wool of her sweater, his urgent fingers burning the tender skin of her midriff.

Greer trembled violently.

She felt him pull away and she reached out blindly, catching his face between her hands, cradling him, feeling the muscles of his jaw move beneath the silken strength of his thick beard.

'Don't stop,' she cried, hoarsely.

'I have to, otherwise . . . I won't be able to, later.' His voice was ragged.

She opened her eyes and gazed in wonder at the face of the man she knew she loved as she had never loved before.

'But I don't want you to stop! I want you to make love to me.' Nothing else mattered, and she had no shame.

'Don't you think I want that too?' His face was tortured, his eyes pools of pain, his sensual mouth drawn downwards. 'But don't you see, we'd only regret it. You'd feel cheap and used . . . afterwards . . . because that's all there'd be. We're not free, either of us, and I don't want you on those terms.'

He wrenched himself from her and stood rigidly, as though fighting emotions she couldn't begin to imagine, while she lay still, feeling the heat of the fire he'd lit in her body die away.

Slowly, she became aware of the way the sun was sliding across the sky, its heat already waning, and she shivered, though the day was still warm.

She heard the soft sound of the horses as they snuffled in the grass, the breeze ruffling the branches above them; the distant tumble of water.

The world went on, and only she was different.

'You're right.' She spoke tonelessly. 'I feel cheap anyway, even though we didn't . . . but because you know you could have made love to me, and I wouldn't have stopped you. You must think I'm — '

Byron wheeled round, fierce as a bandit. 'I don't think you're anything except wonderful and brave, and beautiful and funny. If circumstances were different — but it's no use saying that, because they're not.'

He held out his hand and Greer scrambled to her feet, clinging to his hand as though to a lifeline as her limbs seemed to have lost all strength.

'What made you pull away?' she asked in a whisper. 'I couldn't have stopped if the sky had fallen.' Her eyes were huge and forlorn.

'When you started to shake, you seemed so vulnerable, and it hit me that you aren't as tough as you pretend to be. I couldn't hurt you — and you would have ended up feeling wounded. Your pride, if nothing else.'

'But that's not true! I made the decision. I'm my own person, and I make my own rules. The only reason I was shaking was . . . emotion. Not fear, if that's what you think. I know it's hard for you to accept that a woman could take the initiative.' She looked at him searchingly and saw, with a feeling of despair, that she was only making matters worse.

She could feel him retreating from her and his eyes were becoming distant. 'Oh, Byron, it doesn't make you any less of a man, or me any less of a woman, if I make a decision like that, knowing the consequences.'

'*Your* decision, Greer. It was *your* decision, not mine. And a decision necessarily involving two people.' A sad smile twisted his lips. 'It had to be mutual.'

Greer hung her head, her face

burning. 'So you didn't want to make love to me? I've just been making a fool of myself again?'

He grasped her shoulders, hurting her with his powerful grip. 'I've wanted you since I first met you, but I can't — oh, God, trying not to hurt you, I've hurt you even more.' He was a man in torment.

'You must love her very much,' Greer said in a small voice, and felt his hand slide hopelessly from her.

'You have Steven.' He neither confirmed nor denied her statement.

'Yes.' Feeling lost and lonely, she laid her head for a moment on his shoulder, drinking in the scent of his aftershave, underlaid with a disturbingly masculine skin-smell, partly the light sheen of perspiration, partly unperfumed soap, all combined with the heavy oiled-wool smell.

With a supreme strength of will, she pulled herself away, but he caught and held her, lifting her face to his, which was stern and unsmiling, his strange scar white and taut. 'And do you love him?'

She knew she didn't, but she had to salvage some of that pride he'd mentioned. She was only human after all, and she couldn't let him know just how bereft she was, knowing that, though he might want her physically, his love for another woman was so steadfast he had the strength to refuse her open, flaunted invitation. 'Of course I do,' she assured him, brightly. 'But we have a relationship that allows us each to do our own thing. I'm sure he must have the odd flirtation now and then as well.'

'So that's what this is to you? Fun? A way of passing the time?' He drew away from her and she flinched at the condemnation in his expression. 'I should have taken you, shouldn't I?' he snarled. 'Physical gratification, that's all it would have meant to you, and I'm sure I'd have found it very satisfying too. Well, find somebody else to be your plaything, not me!'

He was so hopelessly wrong, but perhaps it was better if he thought that. Better than him knowing her true feelings. At least that way she could hide the pain.

And he'd obviously never try to make love to her again, which was just as well. Because she knew she'd never be able to refuse him if he did.

5

He subjected her to a view of his back, haughty and cold, during their ride to the inn, and when they finally arrived she disappeared into the 'Ladies' for an inadequate grooming session. 'Though why I waste my time,' she said to her dishevelled mirror-image, 'I don't know. If I was grooming a horse, he'd undoubtedly appreciate it!'

'I've ordered home-made celery soup and a ploughman's,' he informed her coldly when she returned to the low-ceilinged bar. 'I hope that's to your liking?'

'A bit late if it isn't,' she murmured as the barmaid emerged with two steaming bowls of soup.

'Sorry. I forgot you're used to wearing the trousers.' Was he being deliberately infuriating, or did it just come naturally?

She decided to ignore him and sat down gingerly on the hard wooden settle. After all, the fresh air and exercise had promoted a healthy appetite and the soup was exceptionally good.

'Damn,' muttered Byron at the sound of a car door being slammed. 'I thought we'd have this place to ourselves.'

'Would you like me to hide under the table?' She was only half joking.

'Don't be ridiculous. I do exactly as I please. The day I start to worry about what others might say . . . No, I just thought we could talk. There are things we should sort out.' He looked at her searchingly, and for a fleeting moment placed his hand over hers. Even that merest of contacts sent sparks flying through her like a bonfire party.

'What sort of things?' Why was her foolish heart hammering so?

But she was not to know.

'Byron! I *thought* that was Forester out there. Not at market today?' A large, rawboned woman who'd entered stared at Greer with undisguised curiosity.

Greer noticed the speed at which Byron drew away from her and felt bereft. 'Fool, fool,' she said to herself, 'you mean nothing to him.'

He unwound himself from the low settle. 'Marjorie! Nice to see you. I sent Alun to market today. Time I had a day off and exercised the horses.'

'Yes, indeed. Won't be long before the hunting season.'

'Er — I don't suppose you know Greer? She's staying at Ty Bach for a few weeks. Sit down and I'll get you a drink — lager, isn't it?'

The woman sat opposite Greer, staring at her in a none-too-polite manner. 'Someone said the cottage was occupied,' she commented as Byron went to the bar, 'but I'd assumed it was Ailsa living there.'

'Ailsa?'

'Yes.' Marjorie lowered her voice as though not wishing Byron to hear her engaged in tittle-tattle. 'They're going to be wed, you know.'

'Ailsa — and Byron?' Greer's appetite suddenly disappeared.

The woman nodded vigorously.

'Why would she move into the cottage? Byron's got his own house, which I should imagine is in a better state than Ty Bach.'

'Only temporary, I mean. And I'm probably jumping the gun, but it'd be the logical conclusion for it all, for those two to get married. She's so lovely, and they've been through so much . . . ' Her eyes misted over at the thought of so much loveliness, unaware that her words were knives in Greer's heart. So — he'd told her he wasn't married, which was true. But he'd omitted to say it was only a matter of time before he was. And he wanted to install the object of his passion in the cottage first.

My cottage, she thought fiercely. What a snake in the grass he was.

Greer shot Marjorie a warning glance as Byron returned. She didn't want him to know they'd been discussing his private affairs.

Marjorie and Byron fell to discussing agriculture and horses in animated fashion, and Greer leant back against the wall, savouring the icy sharpness of her drink, feeling it course through her, giving her a false strength to return to the saddle and home. Home. That was what Ty Bach felt like. But it was going to be Ailsa's home, and Byron would be visiting her there. After Greer had returned to her 'real' life. To her business. And to Steven?

She felt herself being examined minutely by Marjorie, who was taking in the tight jeans, the polished cowboy boots, the clinging bright-yellow sweater, and the Jacqmar scarf with which she'd tied back her hair. Wickedly, she wanted to ask if she approved — how she measured up to Ailsa — but she managed to hold her tongue.

By the time they left, the high spirits with which she'd made the outward journey had deserted her, and even the pleasurable feel of the horse beneath her, the heady clearness of the air and the lowering rays of the sun, couldn't dissipate her feeling of desolation.

Trembling with nerves and fatigue, she finally reached the cottage and a subdued Byron left with the horse-box. It was cheerless inside as the sun finally dipped below the horizon, leaving only a sky as yellow as gold, with the same quality of shimmering opalescence reflecting in all the west-ward facing windows. Too tired and numb to think any more, she lit the fire, and lay on the sofa.

Within minutes she was asleep, in the slumber of the emotionally drained and physically exhausted, and didn't wake until the fire had burned low. Realisation dawned that she should have soaked in a warm bath immediately, as the hard seams of her jeans were biting into the delicate skin of her thighs, and she ached from waist to ankles. She groaned as she stood, and hobbled upstairs to the bathroom.

Gingerly, she peeled off the faded blue denims and found, to her horror, that there were livid red weals on the insides of her knees and just below and above them. Her mind must have been so preoccupied with thoughts of Byron that she hadn't realised how much punishment her body was taking. The only consolation was that her bodily discomfort was taking her mind from her emotional pain.

But by the next day, things were rather more serious.

She could hardly move, and the weals had developed into huge blisters. There was nothing for it but to stay in bed and hope that time would heal her aches and pains — even the nagging one in the region of her heart, which ached just as much as all her other muscles, but from a different cause.

She lay in bed all day, reading, though Mary Queen of Scots' trials and tribulations failed to grab her full attention. She found herself watching the clouds scudding across the sky like sails in a race, daydreaming about Byron and wondering why, of all the men she had met in the course of her busy life, she had to fall in love with probably the most unsuitable, and, worst of all, unavailable one.

The only sounds she heard were the men climbing up and down ladders, hammering and sawing, but they just formed a background to the unreality of it all, and after a while she became oblivious to it.

The sky was darkening to a bruised purple when she became vaguely aware of the front door opening and closing. 'Greer?'

She propped herself up sharply on one elbow at the sound of his voice.

'Byron? I'm up here.' Hastily, she smoothed her tousled tresses and straightened the straps of her broderie anglaise shortie nightdress, cursing herself for not having bothered to get up and dressed — he'd think her a slut on top of all her other shortcomings.

His head appeared tentatively around the door and she pulled the sheet up under her chin as she looked back at him, unaware that she looked like a palely winsome waif with her straggly hair and scrubbed-clean face.

He walked into the room, booted feet heavy on the wooden boards, and advanced towards the bed. Involuntarily, she clutched the sheet even tighter. 'I was worried about you. I've been to the house a couple of times, seeing what the builders were doing, and they said they hadn't seen you about. Are you ill?' His face and voice showed his concern, which seemed genuine.

'Not exactly — just feel as though I've been run over by a steam-roller, is all! I thought I kept myself reasonably fit but I obviously exercise different muscles to those used for riding horses.'

'Oh, God — I'm sorry. What an idiot I am, taking you out all day for your first ride. I didn't even think — I wasn't thinking straight at all — '

He stared at her as though aghast at his own stupidity and thoughtlessness and then, to her horror, sat down on the bed, bringing his vibrant masculinity within inches of her frail near-nakedness. She moved to sit up more, keeping the sheet firmly in her hand, and winced.

'Look — I've got some ointment in the car. I never travel without a case of liniments for the horses. Don't look so alarmed — I won't give you a rub-down with horse-liniment. It so happens that I throw everything in my case, ointment for humans as well as horses. I'll go and get it.'

Before she could protest he was flying down the stairs and was back even before she had a chance to slip out of bed and fetch her wrap.

'Right. Where does it hurt most?' He came bounding into the room, bringing a blast of fresh air with him, and seemed entirely unaware of her discomfiture.

'Can't I rub it in myself?' she quavered.

'Depends where it is, unless you're a contortionist. Oh, I see,' at last he'd noticed her blushes. 'I suppose this could be rather embarrassing. I think you know you can trust me though — after yesterday.'

Greer's cheeks burned redder than ever. Why did he have to remind her what a fool she'd made of herself over him?

'I expect it's just the backs of your legs, is it?' He was trying to be kind to her and she could hardly bear it. Why couldn't he be a bastard, so that she could justifiably try to hate him? She reminded herself of his lies by omission, and steeled herself to look back at him as coolly as she knew how.

'Yes, it is *just* the backs of my legs, as you put it.' She ignored the wicked laughter that lurked in those navy-blue eyes.

'I'll turn my back while you sort

yourself out from this heap of bedclothes,' he said, blithely. 'Then, if you lie on your stomach, I'll rub in the ointment. What could be more innocent than that?'

Nothing, thought Greer, if you were my maiden aunt, or if my blasted hormones didn't react like short-circuited electricity every time you're near.

With unnatural obedience, trying to shut her mind to what was happening, Greer carried out this manoeuvre, moving slowly and carefully so as not to put any more strain on her poor muscles.

'Ready,' she said at last. She'd pulled her nightdress as far down as it would go, but it still only reached mid-thigh. To hell with it, she thought; as Byron said, I know I can trust him, though I doubt his precious Ailsa would believe what we were doing if she walked in on us!

She realised she was putting herself in a vulnerable position but, despite some misgivings, felt reasonably sure that she was safe with Byron.

As he'd bluntly stated . . . 'after yesterday.'

She heard his swift intake of breath as he turned back to her, but it wasn't her irresistible body that caused it, merely the blisters that were now only too plainly visible.

'Why didn't you tell me? You must have been in terrible pain! You should never have ridden back in that state.' His eyes raked her palely luminous body in the fading light of early evening, horrified at the vivid marks that, in places, had turned to blisters and in others were fading to dark bruises.

'We weren't exactly in a chatty mood,' was her slightly muffled reply, and she heard him groan penitently.

And then she felt his fingertips touch the tender skin at the back of her knees. They were cold, and she froze, in more ways than one. She felt the smear of ointment on her skin and his fingers began to move, gently massaging it in.

'There's no need to be nervous,' he assured her, softly.

'I'm not nervous,' she protested, too quickly. 'It's just that your hands are so cold — and this bedroom's none too warm.'

She heard the rustle of clothing, the crackle of electricity as he pulled something off, and then her shoulders and back were smothered in the soft wool of his sweater, still containing the heat of his body and redolent of his cologne.

'Is that better?' At her nod, his hands resumed their work. 'Just relax. Your muscles are like bowstrings. Trust me. Let yourself go. Pretend it's not me doing this, if that helps.'

Impossible, though, to imagine those hands, touching her so intimately yet so impersonally, belonged to anyone but him.

The friction of skin against skin was creating warmth, and the action of the ointment produced a healing heat which began to penetrate to the muscles themselves as he worked his way from mid-thigh down to the bottom of her calf muscles. The touch of his hands was like magic, strong yet delicate in the way he manipulated her muscles and, whilst he behaved with commendable propriety, for Greer the experience was erotically sensuous.

He turned his attention to the other leg and repeated the process so that, by the time he'd finished, Greer was practically swooning with pleasure, though she'd have died rather than let him realise the effect he was having on her.

He had his pride, but she had even more, and the thought of being rejected by him two days running was insupportable.

'That was much more fun than rubbing down a horse,' she heard him say, half to himself. 'Now, where's that salve for the blisters?'

He was sorting through the ancient leather Gladstone in which he kept the medications and Greer watched him warily from the corner of her eye, wanting, yet not wanting, this delicious torment to end.

'Now, ahem, this is going to sound terrible. Could you — ah — part your legs a little more?' She could feel herself blushing right down to the tips of her toes as she spread her legs just enough to allow him to apply, with infinite tenderness, a different ointment to the inflammation around the knee joint.

With delicate care, his fingers strayed to the velvet-soft concavity of her upper thigh, where the blisters ended in a line of pale pink that was only very slightly sore.

'I think,' he cleared his throat, 'that's as far as I dare go, if I'm to remain dispassionate about this.' He patted her bottom through its thin cotton in a casually, friendly manner, but his words and the tone of his voice told Greer that he wasn't unmoved by the close physical contact with her near-naked body.

She smiled grimly to herself, her face hidden from view. This time, he wasn't going to get an open invitation.

'If you'd fetch my wrap from the bathroom, I'll make myself decent and fix some coffee.' She marvelled at how composed she sounded.

'As your medical adviser, I wouldn't dream of allowing you out of bed.' One hand still rested lightly and unthreateningly on the back of her knee and Greer reflected ruefully that she'd never before realised it was one of the erogenous zones.

'You must keep your muscles warm now, so hop back under the covers and I'll make the coffee.' Still his hand lay on her leg and Greer didn't trust herself to move an inch lest in some way their physical contact became even more intimate, however carefully Byron might be avoiding that.

The room was all-but dark now, only a cold white glow from the window keeping it from inky blackness, and she thought what a strange tableau they must make, still as statues, neither daring nor wanting to move, it seemed, as Byron made no attempt to leave.

His hand moved, infinitesimally caressing her smooth skin. 'Like alabaster,' he murmured, almost inaudibly, then, 'No — that's cold and hard, and you're warm . . . soft . . . alive . . . and too damnably enticing.'

He stood abruptly and she heard his footsteps recede to the doorway, where he paused. 'You must think I'm a bloody idiot.' He sounded angry.

'No. Why should I think that?' She turned her head on the pillow but it was too dark to see his expression.

'I imagine most men would have been quick to take advantage of this situation.'

'Then 'most men' would have got a slap round the face,' Greer responded pertly.

She thought it was safe, under cover of darkness, to climb back into bed, and, by the time he returned with two mugs of coffee, she was respectable in his midnight-blue sweater. It swamped her, but, with its high turtle-neck, removed any chance of him accusing her of attempting to seduce him.

'You've lost your sweater temporarily — if I'm to stay in bed and there's no heater up here, my need is greater than yours.'

'It's the least I can do. And besides — you look much better in it.'

She'd switched on the bedside lamp and the wide bed was bathed in a pool of peach-coloured light, the shabby decorations and damp patches no longer visible.

Byron sat down on the bed again. 'You'll need to rest up for a day or two.' He looked at her with quick concern, his dark brows drawn together. 'Will you be all right here? On your own? It's not a place anyone would choose to be cooped up in.'

'I've grown quite attached to it, as a matter of fact. It needs a lot of work done, and the furnishings leave a lot to be desired, but it could be lovely. The sort of weekend retreat a lot of people are after. Why don't you sell it, Byron, then you wouldn't have to worry about it any more?'

She knew she was putting him on the spot, but, sooner or later, she had to know the truth of it all. She had, as much as she was able, come to terms with the fact that he must be very much in love with Ailsa, but what had that woman meant . . . 'it would be a logical conclusion'?

Instinct told her that somehow the cottage was a part of his past that influenced the present, but she was mystified by the undercurrents.

Did Byron, in some way, feel responsible for Ailsa? Did he, perhaps — a tiny flame of hope flaring at the thought — feel he *had* to marry her? There was no denying that he was drawn, physically at least, to Greer, and if he was that much in love with Ailsa —

'It's part of the farm estate.' His voice, carefully emotionless, broke into her thoughts. 'I couldn't sell, even if I wanted to.'

'But it seems to hold such sad memories for you.' Greer spoke softly. For a man so big, so strong, so intelligent, at times he seemed to be racked with a torment over which he had little control.

She knew only too well what torture that could be, from the long lonely years of her childhood and the equally long lonely struggle for success.

'Yes.' Instinctively, his hand went to his scar. He stared into the dark corner of the room seemingly oblivious to her presence.

'Tell me what happened.' Her eyes unexpectedly filled with tears, he seemed to be in such pain. 'How did you get such a scar?'

'In an accident.' She waited, but the silence grew until she began to think that was all he would say.

Abruptly, he began to speak again. 'It was a flying accident. I had a small light aeroplane. Much quicker to get to some of the racecourses that way.' She knew he entered races as far away as Scotland sometimes, and the horses went ahead in their boxes with the head lad. 'There's a small field, not far from here, big enough for that type of light aircraft. I came back one evening . . . it was getting foggy . . . but I took a chance. Thought I could get it down — I knew the field so well. Just bloody obstinate, though, I realise that now, now that it's too late.' His voice broke on his last words and Greer took his hand in hers, seeing the desperate sadness in his deep blue eyes. The strong, broad hand trembled violently in hers and he took a deep, shuddering breath.

'I came down just a bit too late, and couldn't pull her up in time. Ploughed through the fence at the end of the runway and finished up crashing into some trees.'

His head was averted, his shoulders hunched. All Greer could see was the back of his dark, tousled head, the check shirt collar turned up untidily, the broad plane of his shoulder. It had cost him a great effort of will to relive the tragedy.

Leaning back against the pillows, Greer imagined the dreadful noise of the crash. The cold terror he must have felt. The final rending of the small aircraft. The panic, waiting for it to burst into flames. Trying to free himself from the wreckage before it did.

'But you were so lucky,' she breathed, 'to escape with just a scar — unless — did you have any other injuries?'

'Oh, I was lucky, that's true.' His voice was even grimmer. 'Just a couple of cracked ribs and a bit of concussion, apart from this gash. Luckier than my brother.'

'Your brother? I didn't know you had a brother?' I know as little about you as the day we first met, except that you possess my heart.

'I don't have a brother. Not any more. Forgive me — I'm telling this very badly. I hardly ever talk about it.

It's something I have nightmares about, even now, though it happened over two years ago. My brother died, you see. Because of me and my pig-headedness.'

His deep voice was anguished and he dropped his head into his hands. Greer leant forward, throwing her arms around him, dragging him bodily towards her, until she felt him sag against her, his head on her shoulder. For the first time, she felt stronger than him, and she was overwhelmed by a tenderness she never knew she possessed.

'As you said,' she whispered, 'it was an accident. They happen. You can't blame yourself for ever — you can't live with that kind of guilt.'

'But you don't understand.' He raised his head and his eyes, inches from her own, glistened unashamedly with unshed tears. 'It wasn't as simple as that. He — Liam, my brother — pulled Ailsa and myself from the plane — '

'Ailsa? She was on board, too?' Greer

couldn't stop her exclamation, but he seemed not to hear her —

' — and came with us in the ambulance to the hospital.'

'So he wasn't killed in the crash? I thought you said — '

'No. He stayed until he knew we were both going to survive, then he went to attend to the stock and reassure my mother. After that, he came back here, to the cottage.' Bryon's face was bleak and pale under his tan, and she ached for him.

It seemed difficult for him to resume, but when he did she understood at last just why he hadn't set foot in the place for years. Why the house had been so neglected. Why it was haunted by such terrible memories for him.

'The doctors at the hospital had been so preoccupied with Ailsa and myself — and it's only a cottage hospital manned by the local GPs, who are overstretched anyway — that they didn't even examine Liam. No blame can be attached to them, though — I mean, he was walking about, saying he was fine.'

'What happened?'

Byron shook his head despairingly. 'People told us we should have sued, but what was the point? It wouldn't have brought him back. Anyway, Dr Davies has looked after us all our lives. It wasn't his fault.' He cleared his throat, on the edge of breaking down.

'Liam died here, in this cottage. On his own. He had internal injuries, but he didn't collapse until he'd seen to everything, and everyone, else. It should have been me who died; me, the selfish, self-centred brother, not him.'

'Don't be so hard on yourself,' Greer admonished him, stroking his springy, tangled hair. What strength of character it must have taken for him ever to set foot in the place again. 'You're a caring person and you don't appear particularly selfish to me.'

'Because you've only known me as I am now.' The set of his mouth was grim. 'Before . . . I was the proverbial black sheep. Wild and irresponsible. I didn't want to go into farming, so Liam ran the farm, while I started up my own racing-stables. That was just an excuse, though, to get involved in the racing game. And that's what it was to me — a game. I didn't make any money; in fact, I was losing it hand over fist, and being bailed out by Liam all the time. Not any more, though. Now I work in deadly earnest and it's beginning to pay off. But all the hard work doesn't bring Liam back, it only helps assuage my conscience a little. I can pay for the farm to employ people, keep my mother and run the farmhouse . . . the things I left for Liam to see to. I suppose, without wishing to sound melodramatic, I decided to take Liam's place . . . in everything.'

'At whatever cost to yourself?'

He drew away from her, holding her at arm's length. He looked drained, yet more at peace. Perhaps the reliving of such a traumatic event had helped him to come to terms with what had happened.

'Yes. Whatever it costs me, it will never make up for Liam's life.'

He stood up with immeasurable weariness. 'So now you know what it cost me to come back here, to be reminded all over again of what happened.'

'I'm sorry, Byron. I made that awful crack about someone dying here — '

'You weren't to know, and I shouldn't have been so rude to you. But now you do know, you'll forgive me if I don't come here again, won't you?' He looked around at the shadowed room. 'It's still haunted for me, and I can't escape the past. I realise that even more, now.'

And I seem to have become linked with that past, thought Greer, with dread. No matter what happens in the future, I'll always remind him of this cottage, and his dead brother.

'You mentioned someone called Ailsa.' She didn't tell him she already knew about her from other lips.

He looked down at her, his expression unfathomable.

'Ailsa is the girl I'm going to marry,' he said, simply. 'Didn't I tell you?'

6

Hours later, Greer rose wearily from the wreckage of her lonely bed, wondering if she would ever sleep again.

Stiffly, she walked to the window, shivering slightly in the chill night air, and leant on the cold stone. Byron had been right in his initial estimation of her. She had been a stupid, egocentric child. She was so sure she could conquer the world, and what did she truly know about the one thing that really mattered — human relationships?

Nothing!

She'd always been so busy that the only reason there'd been any space in her life for Steve was because he was her accountant. What had she given him of herself?

Nothing!

And then, like a spoiled child, she'd

thought she could have Byron, just because she wanted him. But he was a man of a different calibre from any other she'd known. He'd survived disaster and tragedy, and emerged as tempered steel. She'd thought she was tough, but now she knew she shared the same frailty as every other woman.

She was a victim of her own emotions.

Finally, she had come to terms with the fact that Byron would never be hers. She felt a sharp stab of pain — envy, jealousy? — at the thought that he would belong to Ailsa. Does she love him as much as I do, she wondered, and then 'How could she not?' said a small, chilling voice in her head. She'd agreed to spend the rest of her life with him, hadn't she?

In desperation, she tried to turn her mind to other thoughts, to stop her head from spinning and her mind from churning over and over. Her eyes searched the darkness for an owl she could hear but not see.

She touched her mouth with delicate fingers, as though not wishing to disturb the soft creases where Byron's mobile lips had momentarily burnt against hers. It had astonished her. After all the revelations about the accident, the tragedy of his brother's death, and the fact that he was to marry Ailsa, Greer had lain there devastated, unable even to offer words of comfort.

In a haze of her own misery, she couldn't stop wondering why he'd been so furious with her when he'd thought she was fooling around with him. Obviously, that was all he'd been doing with her. She couldn't be angry with him, though. She was too full of misery and concern for him. Perhaps anger would come later.

But where is the mysterious Ailsa, she wondered? I wouldn't let him run loose around the countryside if he was mine. And why, oh why, did he have to go and kiss me goodnight?

She glimpsed a movement — the silhouette of the owl as it left the shelter of the barn — and she watched the outline of its broad span of wings cross the moon-flooded meadow until it disappeared into the dense darkness of the wood.

She shivered again. Even the sound of the owl had been company, but now she was alone again.

True to his word, Byron stayed strictly away from the cottage — and from her. Being young, strong and healthy, Greer quickly recovered from her ordeal by horseback, but decided to explore by car for a few days, and her excursions took her further afield.

She didn't quite know why she stayed. After all, her decision about Steve had been made, and there was no alternative for her but to go back to work and hope that, in time, the ache in her heart would heal as completely as the aches in her body. Perhaps she needed a little more time for contemplation. For some inner soul-searching.

She'd been touched by the depth of feeling Byron had displayed for his brother, and thought wistfully of her own lack of family. Of course, she still had her mother, but how much thought had she given her of late? Oh, she'd given her a job, that was true. As supervisor of some of the outside catering, where a team of waitresses had to be kept in line. Her mother had proved herself, and was well liked by the staff for whom she was responsible. But was she happy? It hadn't been her fault that she'd left Greer so much when she was young. In fact, she'd worked herself to a shadow in order that Greer should be educated.

Greer thought guiltily of the fact that she'd seen so little of her mother outside working hours. Whatever else happened in her life from now on, she vowed, she'd try to become closer to her mother. If that was the only change to come about as a result of her self-imposed exile, it would be something.

On her own, she drove around enjoying the vast open expanse of countryside, visiting ancient ruined border castles at Chepstow, Raglan and Abergavenny, and wandering amongst the sprinkling of other late visitors, camera in hand. She even went shopping for green wellingtons, a Barbour jacket and heavy cord jeans, wondering even as she fished out her credit card whether she'd ever wear them again.

She found herself turning to the sports page of her daily newspaper, something she'd never done in her life, but it was the racing page that suddenly proved fascinating, providing a tenuous link with Byron's activities. Even seeing his name printed made her heart leap, and she followed his fortunes avidly, looking eagerly the next day to discover if any of the previous day's runners had been placed.

Then, one clear morning, which had more than a hint of winter to come in its brisk east wind, she saw that he had horses entered at Ludlow, and hurried out to her car for the map. It wasn't far.

She'd never been racing, so why not remedy that gap in her education?

Of course she didn't expect to see Byron. He'd be too busy anyway. And, besides, surely he'd take Ailsa with him, as the course was so near to home. Perhaps she'd be able to view her from a distance, then at least she'd have an image on which to focus her envy.

She approached the course over a rutted track across the fields, and paid to go in the members' enclosure. The little course was humming with activity. Men in sharp hats were preoccupied with marking their programmes, consulting the *Sporting Life* with worried expressions. Bookmakers waved their arms in extraordinary fashion, shouting the odds. Women dressed to the nines, teetering on unsuitably high heels, wore gooseflesh as well, in the teeth of what had become a gusting near-gale in the flat, unsheltered expanse.

The horses appeared to be almost incidental to everything else that was happening, and to get to the paddock

Greer had to cross the race-track in between the second and third races. Byron had a horse entered in the next race, she'd noted, by the exotic name of Pampered Princess.

The horses were parading in the paddock, their aristocratic breeding evident in every line of their tautly-muscled bodies, and Greer leant on the rail, admiring the gleaming chestnuts, the glossy bays, and the solitary grey, dramatic with a scarlet blanket. The jockeys, colourful in their racing silks, were engaged in conversation with owners and trainers.

Greer saw Byron before he spotted her.

Standing half a head taller than anyone else on the brilliant green turf, he seemed to diminish the stature of everyone around him. Clad in a casually expensive herring-bone tweed coat, its collar upturned against the cold, he was talking animatedly, his hands thrust in deep pockets, to a jockey.

Greer's eyes were riveted on him. She thought, this is the last time I'll ever see him, and wondered at herself for being so pathetic. Whatever had happened to Greer Jameson, successful business-woman?

The sooner I get back to London the better, she scolded herself, if I'm to be reduced to peering at him from afar. Wanting him. Knowing I can't have him.

As if aware of her scrutiny, Byron raised his eyes, and looked straight into hers. The shock was mutual. Greer hadn't expected him to notice her, in the sea of faces, and it was obvious that he found her sudden appearance baffling. She watched as he placed a friendly hand on the jockey's shoulder, evidently cutting short their conversation, and strode in her direction.

'I didn't know horse-racing numbered amongst your interests!' His eyes hadn't left her face since he'd spotted her.

'It isn't — wasn't. It . . . it's

colourful, isn't it?' She was stammering and blushing like a teenager.

'I suppose so.' Now his eyes travelled in a downward direction, and a slow smile lit his face. 'I see you took my advice then.'

'Fortunately — the jacket may not be the last word in glamour but it keeps out the cold, and the boots are rather more sensible than the type I usually wear, but they're much more suitable for this type of event. I don't look that comical, do I?' she asked crossly, as he was laughing outright, his eyes reflecting the light of the sky.

'No. You look wonderful — as always. I'm flattered that I should have that much influence on you.'

'It wasn't just you. It became rather obvious that my usual wardrobe wasn't exactly appropriate,' she said, haughtily, and Byron nodded.

'I'm delighted to see you, anyway, whatever you're wearing. Er — all the bruises gone, have they? And the blisters, they've healed?'

Greer avoided his eyes, feeling her skin grow warm again in remembrance. 'Yes, the patient made a speedy recovery, thanks to your ministrations. I've been dashing about all over the place, so I thought I'd see what it was like going to the races.' She didn't want him to think she'd come here specifically to see him.

'I'm glad you did. Look, I have to go. They'll be off to the start in a minute and I've got another horse in the fifth race, so I'll be busy.'

'Yes, of course. Don't let me keep you.' Greer went to turn away but he reached over and caught her by the shoulder.

'I didn't mean — it's just that I've things to do. But I do want to see you afterwards. Will you wait for me? I'll be able to get away then, and I'll meet you in the members' bar, if that's OK with you?'

Greer hesitated momentarily. She'd tried all week to banish him from her thoughts. Was it wise to permit even a chink in the armour she'd built around herself, so painfully, all week?

'We could have dinner somewhere afterwards. You don't have to hurry back, do you?' His voice was persuasive, and the temptation to share a meal, and an evening, with him, was irresistible.

Why punish herself unnecessarily? It would only be an evening out with a friend, and no harm done

'You've talked me into it,' she smiled, while the sun, deceptively bright, came out from behind a cloud that resembled a sheet of grey metal.

True to his word, he met her in the bar, and insisted on buying a bottle of champagne, to celebrate a win. 'Pampered Princess. She's obstinate, stubborn and wilful — rather like someone I know,' he mocked, 'but she's a winner!'

'In that she resembles me as well.' Greer held out her glass of foaming golden liquid and touched his.

'Touché!' He made a mock bow.

'Here's to both the pampered princesses in my life,' and her heart missed a beat.

The air of euphoria stayed with him all through dinner, Greer having had to follow his black Jensen ('It's old, but they don't make 'em like that any more') at limit-breaking speeds through a grey dismal dusk, until they parked in a narrow side-street where a brightly-lit sign proclaimed an Italian trattoria.

The food was excellent, authentically Italian in flavour and content, the wine fruity and fullbodied, and the company sparkling.

Greer had never seen Byron so elated.

He explained, 'That filly had been virtually written off. She was so nervous and over-excitable the previous trainer advised the owners to sell her. They didn't, though — they brought her to me, and now they're over the moon. She's got class, and it shows in the end. She belongs to a syndicate so, with any luck, they'll be changing trainers for all their horses. It's not just the additional business, though — it's the pleasure I get from seeing a horse come good after all the hard work.'

'You enjoy it, don't you?' Greer looked over the rim of the wineglass. 'The excitement, the lifestyle.'

'I could never have stayed on the farm the rest of my life, that's true. I'd have got introspective and moody in my old age.'

'You mean you're not already?' Greer exclaimed, teasingly.

'Uh, uh.' He shook his head. 'You're the one doing the introspective bit. How's it going? Have you made any momentous decisions? Are you going to play house with Steve when you get back?' His hand lay on the table, and she noticed it tense a little.

'Yes, I have.' It seemed their relationship had reached a stage where they could be honest with each other. He had become a friend, and she was in need of a friend.

'I realise I don't love him, so I'm

going to tell him, no.' She heard Byron's slight exhalation of breath. 'I — I like him, but that's not enough, is it?' She looked at Byron earnestly, and knew the answer to her own question. Now if Byron had asked her . . .

'Not nearly enough.' He reached forward and took her hand, turning it and raising it to his lips. Gently, he kissed the delicate skin of her inner wrist and she trembled. 'I know I'm selfish, but I'm glad you made that decision. And I think you're right. You've been here for weeks, and he's left you strictly alone. I couldn't have done that, if I'd been in his shoes.'

'But I asked him to, and he's just respecting my wishes.' Greer pulled her hand away. She could so easily succumb to Byron's charms and she suspected they were nearing a danger zone. In his present mood she felt he was capable of saying and doing anything, no matter how outrageous.

'Wouldn't you — just sometimes — like to have a man around who didn't respect your wishes? Who told you what you were damn well going to do and what *he* was going to do? Wouldn't you prefer a real man to a doormat?'

'Steve's anything but a doormat, I can assure you. And no, I don't need to be dominated. I know a lot of women do, but I just don't happen to be one of them.' Her eyes sparkled in the candlelight as she looked at him challengingly. 'I thought I'd already made that clear to you.'

'Oh, you've gone out of your way to do so — but sometimes I think you protest too much. Perhaps you should try it some time.' His tone was relaxed, but Greer had the feeling he was testing the ground in some way, and her guard was up.

When they eventually left, though, and she held out a polite hand to wish him goodnight, he ignored it and put both his hands on her shoulders.

'You're coming back to my place. For a coffee and a glass of Amoretto. You have to finish an Italian meal with that, it's compulsory! Besides, it would be such an anticlimax for me to finish the evening alone.'

It wasn't until she was following his tail-lights back that she wondered why Ailsa wasn't with him. Why Ailsa couldn't share his coffee and liqueur. Why she could never say 'no' to him.

Perhaps the truth of it was that her curiosity had overcome her. The opportunity to see him in his own environment was appealing.

She followed him through a wide gateway and into a courtyard. An ancient stone building of massive proportions formed one side of the yard, a grey bulk silhouetted against the sky, all its many windows dark and closed. At the far end stood a long low outbuilding, lost in the shadows and, opposite the main house, a stable-block, its mellowed brickwork illuminated by the lights of Byron's car. She parked beside him and he opened her door with a flourish.

'Welcome to Penybank Farm.' But he led her towards the stable-block. Opening a stable-type door, they entered a functional modern office, complete with desk-top computer and word-processor. It was so unexpected in this rural setting that Greer could only stand and stare. 'Is this where you work?'

'No, it's where my secretary works,' said Byron, with a quirk of his brow, 'and it's not what I brought you here to see.' He nodded towards a wrought-iron spiral staircase, indicating that she should precede him upwards. It seemed about as hazardous as picnicking on the lip of a volcano, but she went without demur.

A huge room, its gleaming polished floorboards scattered with rugs, lay before her. Dormer windows looked out onto the cobbled yard and the dark mass of the main house. At one end was a vast modern picture-window and the room itself was a pleasing mixture of old and new, with voluptuous sofas of off-white leather, low-slung lamps hung strategically, and simple blinds at the windows. A lattice-fronted bookcase stood against one wall, while an illuminated corner-cupboard held a display of what she guessed to be a valuable collection of porcelain vases and figures.

'You obviously don't keep your horses in the stables, nor hay in your hayloft!' She turned to find him much too close for comfort and she walked away to stare out at the total darkness.

'No, they're out there.' He'd followed her and pointed out to a faint glimmer of light. 'And the gallops are beyond them. I can stand here naked on the coldest day and watch them working out, timing them to a split second,' he stated, and Greer smiled involuntarily.

'That conjures up quite a picture. I wonder what your lads would say if they could see you.'

'Hm, well, fortunately I have complete privacy here.' He looked at her sidelong and her nervousness increased.

'Where's this coffee you promised?' She stepped backwards, not noticing a low stool, and stumbled.

'Careful!' He caught her round the waist and steadied her, and she was aware of that wonderful combination of cologne, soap, horses and wool that clung to him. Would she ever banish it from her memory?

'What are you going to do?' he asked, not letting go.

'Do? What do you mean?' She could feel her pulses racing.

'If you're not going to marry Steve? You're not just going to become a hard-bitten career-woman, are you? Getting tougher and tougher as the years go on? That would be such a waste.'

'Why should you care? You've got Ailsa, after all.' She stared at him, her eyes darkening challengingly.

'Why should I care? I don't know why, when you're always so damnably defensive.' He almost pushed her from him, and his mood changed in an instant. 'Let's have that drink. Driving back, I'd decided to open a bottle of Moet et Chandon I'd put in the 'fridge in readiness. I had a feeling about Pampered Princess — and *she* didn't let me down.' He looked at her accusingly.

'With whom were you intending to share it, then?' Greer flashed. 'You didn't know you'd bump into me. Don't tell me you were going to celebrate all alone.'

'No, I'd have probably rounded up some friends — but I didn't need to, once I had your company.'

While Byron opened the champagne, Greer sat, rather primly, in an armchair, rather than a sofa, feeling there'd be less opportunity for him to be near her.

It wasn't Byron she didn't trust. It was herself.

To her dismay, though, he lowered himself onto the arm of the chair, leaning across her to pour a stream of sparkling bubbles into their glasses. 'Drink that, and for God's sake, relax.

You look like a Sunday-school teacher in that get-up — don't you think you could remove the wellington boots at least?'

Greer giggled. She took a gulp of wine and felt the bubbles fizz inside her head. Why worry about anything, she thought, kicking off her boots and stretching her legs luxuriously.

'That's better.' She lay back against the smooth leather and took another swallow. 'Um, this is good stuff. I do love champagne, don't you?'

'Only when I share it with a pretty girl.'

'If I didn't know you better, I'd say you were flirting with me.'

'I've never been able to perfect that particular art, but then I haven't had a lot of practice.'

'I find that hard to believe. There must have been lots of women in your life.'

He shrugged. 'Some.' Infuriatingly non-committal. His arm slid along the back of her chair and she could feel his warm breath stirring the tendrils of pale hair on her forehead.

'Greer,' his voice was deep and a little unsteady, 'I don't know if I'm on my head or my heels, wanting you so much.'

'Wanting me?' Greer took another long drink of champagne, as though the cool liquid would help clear the confusion in her head, but it only served to make matters worse. What was he saying? That he wanted her. Well, of course he did, she knew that. But that was all it was. He had Ailsa.

'I wish I could stop.' He sounded anguished. 'I wish we'd never met.'

'I don't.' Greer twisted round and looked him full in the eyes. 'If I hadn't met you, I might never have known that I'm capable of . . . such a depth of feeling. Yes, it hurts, because of Ailsa.' Her eloquent expression implored him to deny Ailsa's place in his life, in his heart, and his face revealed his own pain. 'But even if all this . . . you and I . . . is just a dream

. . . it's better than nothing.'

'Do you really mean that?' His voice was so low she hardly heard him but she nodded emphatically. 'Even though you know I'm going to marry Ailsa, you want to share the little time we have? Knowing that I can't offer you anything more?'

'I don't believe you love Ailsa, not as a man should love the woman he's going to marry, but I'm not going to cross-examine you about it. You have your reasons, and I know from painful experience that you're not easily deflected once you've come to a decision.' Greer gave a shaky laugh. 'All I know is I want you every bit as much as you want me.'

Byron groaned and then his mouth captured hers, making her a prisoner of her own passion. Everything else in the world receded except her need for him, and his desire for her.

When he picked her up, as though she was as insubstantial as thistledown, and carried her, like a sacrifice to love, through a low door into the bedroom, she uttered not a word of protest.

She knew she loved him. That was all that mattered.

* * *

Greer awoke next morning to the sun streaming in as a curtain was pulled back and for a second her memory was blank.

Then it all came flooding back to her, as Byron advanced towards the bed, bearing two steaming mugs of coffee.

'We never did have that coffee and Amaretto.' His face was clear and tranquil. It was the first time she'd seen him so at peace with himself and the world.

'No, we didn't.' She shook her head and found it ached sharply. She must have consumed more alcohol than she'd realised. 'What time is it?' She felt strangely shy with him.

He glanced at his watch — which was all he was wearing — and said 'Only

6.30, but it's market-day today, so I'll be wearing my farmer's hat! You can stay here, though. Nobody will bother you — that I can guarantee.'

She looked away from him. 'I'll get back to the cottage, as soon as I'm showered and dressed.'

'Look at me!' His voice brooked no refusal and she reluctantly laid her head back on the pillows and met his eyes. 'I shouldn't have let it happen, should I? Don't look so hurt, my darling — my conscience will never let me rest if you look at me so accusingly.'

'I don't mean to. I just feel sad, that's all — and you didn't 'let it happen'. It takes two, as they say!' She tried to smile but her lips trembled. 'Don't blame yourself for something in which I was an all-too-willing accomplice.'

'It was wonderful, wasn't it?' His voice throbbed with emotion and, at her barely visible nod, he fell upon her with a sound that was halfway between agony and ecstasy. When he finally drew away the light of the day dazzled her as she gazed at him in a daze of love.

'Your eyes are the colour of the sky,' he murmured, his finger tracing her full lower lip, 'and your mouth is the door to heaven.'

'I didn't know you could be so poetic,' she breathed.

'I never have been, till now. You inspire me! Worse than that — you distract me. If I had you in my bed every morning, there'd be no work done around here.'

So saying, he bounded from the bed. 'I wish I could spend the day with you, my darling, but — ' He spread his hands helplessly, then grabbed a large scarlet towel which he proceeded to wrap around himself. 'I must take a shower and leave you.'

Greer watched him as he strode jauntily into the bathroom, wondering why he was so full of joy, and she was so full of sadness. Why don't you say you love me, she wanted to beg him; tell me you love me before you go and then, even if it's not for ever, I'll have something to hang on to?

But all she heard was the sound of him singing in the shower and the whinnying of the horses in the yard.

7

Greer lay in the steamy, scented water in Byron's bathroom, her outline pale and blurred beneath the soapy, pine-tinged depths, imagining that if she turned her head he'd still be there, rubbing his dark curls, admiring her with bold eyes. Her fingers trailed through the water, reliving the way they'd stroked the curled hair against his warm skin.

But the truth was that he'd gone, rushed away without a word of where or when he'd see her again. Her heart lay heavy as stone and it required an enormous effort of will for her to rise, the water falling off her in a shower of silvered droplets in the sunshine.

She dressed in the heavy sweater and cords, pulling on the wellington boots with a grimace. Whatever had become of the elegant Ms Jameson?

Wondering if she'd encounter anyone, she ran down the narrow stairs with more nonchalance than she was feeling, and was glad she had, for there, taking the cover off the typewriter, was a slender woman dressed in checked shirt and neat trousers.

'Goodness, you made me jump!'

'Sorry — I just came to see Mr Meredith about the cottage.' At the woman's puzzled look she elaborated, 'I'm the tenant of Ty Bach.'

'Ah. Poor you! It can't be much of a holiday with builders swarming all over the place. If Byron had told me he intended letting the place, I'd have made sure it was more habitable. These men . . . ' She raised her eyebrows, indicating their ineffectualness in general, and Greer warmed to her.

'I have to admit, I was hopping mad about the state of the place at first, but, well — now that I know the reason. He's told me about his brother,' she added, at the woman's look of enquiry.

'It's taking him a long while to get

over that. Sometimes I wonder if he'll ever be the old Byron again,' she sighed.

'Is he so different then?'

'Different? How different are chalk and cheese? He was never here, before; tearing around the country, breaking hearts from John O'Groats to Land's End. But now — it's as if he's got to punish himself, and he drives everyone else along at his pace, which is frantic at times! Still, we all love him to pieces, so we let him have his way.' She shrugged with a smile of indulgence on her face. 'Mind you, he's been even less himself just lately.' She eyed Greer shrewdly, and Greer hoisted her jacket over her shoulders with feigned indifference.

'How do you mean?'

'On a *very* short fuse. It's as though . . . he's bottling too much inside himself, and he's been taking it out on us! Still, he seemed more cheerful this morning, when I saw him in the yard. Gave me a big hug and said he was sorry he's been such a bear.' She laughed reminiscently. 'You can forgive him anything, can't you?' Her devotion to him was obvious and Greer, who knew how difficult it is to strike that balance between affection and respect in one's employees, could only nod and murmur assent.

'I'll be off, then.'

'Did you get your problems sorted out? About the cottage?'

'Oh — oh, yes. Everything's fine, don't worry,' and she hurried away, hoping nobody was aware that her car had been parked in the cobbled courtyard all night.

She was restless and disinclined to go back to the cottage, so she drove into the small market-town which was the hub of the local community, forgetting, until she arrived, that it was market-day.

It seemed the entire population of the surrounding countryside had decided to go to town. In the high-roofed market hall a babble of voices rose into the haze of fogged sunshine under the glazed roof. Creamy-white cauliflowers were piled high, next to succulent carrots and shiny-skinned onions. There were neatly placed rows of fish; rainbow trout gleaming irridescently, mackerel, plump and speckled, and sprats like silver slithers. Compared to the supermarkets in which she usually shopped, the food was so real, so simple, shopping seemed a pleasure, rather than a chore.

She wandered a little, hoping the early-morning crowd would disperse, and then left the market hall, drawn, rather reluctantly, to the sounds of the cattle-market. She was afraid she'd be distressed at the sight of animals being bought and sold, but it was all part of rural life. The penned sheep, though, looked stoical rather than scared, and the cattle weren't unduly panicky. She supposed they were used to the scene, as were the farmers who stood, heads together in deep discussion, smoking evil-smelling tobacco, or milling around the Market Tavern, which appeared to be serving beer even so early in the day.

It's like stepping back into the past, she thought. Everyone seemed to know everyone else and observed the rituals with which they'd been familiar all their lives. She felt detached as she stood in the archway that led back to the market hall, and wondered if she could ever become part of it.

Her eyes strayed back and forth, absorbing the sights and sounds until suddenly their movement stopped. Everything in her seemed to come to an abrupt halt. Her heart, her lungs, her brain, ceased to function.

Some distance away, on the other side of the sheep-pens, was Byron, holding the hand of a small boy. A boy who, even from afar, was so like him as to be himself when small. The same wild, dark hair, the deep-set eyes, the firm line of jaw. Even the same quirky smile as he looked up at the woman standing on his other side.

Greer's eyes, which had been riveted to Byron and the boy, turned with dread to the woman.

It must be, it had to be, Ailsa. She was smaller than Greer had imagined, frail in contrast with the robust characters surrounding her, and her long, near-black hair was drawn away from her face, the centre parting giving her the austere beauty of a ballerina. And she *was* beautiful.

The woman tossed her head, laughing at something, and her pale face was transformed, her lips widening over perfect teeth and her eyes crinkling.

As in the moment when great injury is inflicted, no pain is felt, so Greer was numb. To witness the man she loved as the central figure in a small family group was unendurable.

She shrank into the shadows, not having the power to move and yet desperately anxious not to be seen. What would he do? Introduce her as his tenant? Meet my son, he'd say; did I tell you I have a son?

No, you didn't, Byron Meredith. You carefully avoided any mention of him.

Perhaps you didn't think it would matter to me, that there was a small replica of yourself walking this earth — the child, presumably, of Ailsa.

The nightmare continued as she watched Byron speak to the woman, who nodded, and they turned to walk away.

Another shock reverberated through her. The woman leaned heavily on a stick but, even with its assistance, she still limped badly, which lent a touch of pathos to her slight, slender body.

This was the catalyst that Greer needed. She took to her heels and ran. Away from the market, away from the crowds. Not stopping until she reached the outskirts of the town and found herself beside a river that tumbled and chuckled along.

By then she was sobbing. Not only had Ailsa borne him a son but she'd also, Greer guessed, sustained permanent injury from the air crash. The ties that bound him to Ailsa were insurmountable.

If only he'd told her, she would never have allowed herself to become so utterly and completely bound up in him.

She walked, slowly now, beside the river. Trying to compose herself and to allow some of the tranquil calm of her surroundings to filter through, but she was in too much torture.

What had scarcely begun, was already over. In her deepest subconscious she'd hoped — for what? Some kind of commitment from Byron, some kind of acknowledgement of his feelings for her?

She could never trust herself to see him again, because she'd scream and shout and recriminate and, in truth, without justification. He'd never promised her anything and it was only her foolish heart that had wished for more.

If he'd been less than truthful with her, well, at what stage should he have told her that he had a child with Ailsa? He'd told her Ailsa had been injured in the plane crash, but hadn't elaborated.

The sight of her, beautiful and brave, damaged yet courageous, was seared into Greer's brain, as was the face of the child. The mirror-image of Byron. With humiliating clarity, Greer realised what an interloper she was.

She'd allowed herself the indulgence of falling in love and she only had herself to blame. Byron had certainly never asked her to do so. Had never made any demands on her other than ones she was only too willing to accede to.

And now it all had to end. Had already ended.

She fought back the bitter bile that rose in her throat and walked on, unseeing, beside the sun-spangled water that ran through the golden valley. I must go away, she thought. Cut short my holiday and leave before there's any danger of Byron turning up. A small, dry sob escaped her at the thought but she wheeled round and hurried back to the town to where her car was parked beneath the castle wall, praying that she wouldn't bump into Byron. She knew she couldn't face him. Not yet. Not ever.

Every small boy she saw made her stare. Had she been imagining it? Maybe he wasn't so much like Byron? But she saw other children, just as dark, with similar features, and none of them had that indefinable familial resemblance of a father and son that she had recognised in that boy's face.

She had reached her car and was just about to start the engine when she caught sight of the woman and the boy rounding the corner, heading for a nearby ice-cream van. There was no sign of Byron so she waited, wanting, for some reason, to have her worst fears confirmed.

They drew level with the car, the boy hopping, skipping and jumping, as the woman moved more slowly. Closer up, Greer realised she was probably only about the same age as herself, but the severe hairstyle, the pallor of her skin, and the slight impediment to her movements, gave the impression of someone older, graver.

'Mummy, Mummy,' the small boy cried. 'Can I have a piece of chocolate in the top?'

'No, I said — just an ordinary one, so let's not have any nonsense,' said the woman in a lilting Welsh accent.

Greer drove away, her heart heavy as a gravestone. The sunshine mocked her with its gaudiness, and she worked herself up into a state of justifiable anger. 'He's a bastard,' she said aloud, 'deceiving that poor woman, neglecting his child. Just to fool around with me. He used me, that's what he did. Oh, I wish — I wish I could hate him!'

It only took her minutes to pack and she left the cottage in a cloud of dust as the wheels skidded on the driveway.

She'd been home a couple of hours when the phone began to ring.

She stood stock-still, staring at the instrument, which lay beside the bronze art nouveau figure on her bedside table, and let it ring. As soon as it stopped she reached down and pulled the plug from its socket. It had to be Byron, nobody else knew she was home, and he was only guessing.

She ached all over with physical and mental exhaustion, for which the only remedy was a hot bath and a couple of sleeping-pills, and, though she awoke next morning with a feeling of dread, she was, on the surface anyway, her old self by the time she set out for the office.

No point in hanging around moping. Work was the best panacea she knew.

Heads turned as she walked into the office-block. She knew she looked terrific, with her hair drawn off her face and piled in a gleaming coil. Heavy silver ear-rings swung against her cheeks and she wore her favourite charcoal-grey tailored suit.

She knew something was wrong, however, the minute she stepped into her office. 'Miss Jameson! Thank goodness! I didn't expect you back yet, but am I pleased to see you.' Rosanna, her secretary, pushed back her chair and hurried across the expanse of mushroom-coloured carpet. Her confusion and distress were obvious.

'Rosanna! Whatever's the matter?'

The girl's pretty face reddened, and she looked down at the floor. 'We — we've lost a couple of our big accounts, and there've been a few other problems.'

'What on earth's been going on? Whose accounts have we lost?' Even as she spoke, Greer was reaching for the phone. There must have been some misunderstanding. She'd spent years building up the business and took endless pains to keep the customers happy. She knew her prices were competitive, her product first-class and the service second to none. Everyone she employed was a professional who took pride in their work.

'Faber and Thornton's was one — '

'No!' Greer stared in horrified amazement. They were one of her most prestigious clients. 'And who else?'

'The outside catering contract for the Britannia Boat Show. Oh, I'm sorry — if only I could have got in touch with you. But Mr Hicks said to leave it all to him, and I wasn't to worry — '

'Mr Hicks? What's Steve got to do with all this?'

'Well, he more or less moved in. Said he'd handle everything. He wouldn't even let me open the mail.' She swallowed, close to tears. 'Mary had to bring the invoices in for him to check before they were posted, and when he saw the one for Faber's he asked why they'd been given a special discount. Mary told him you'd authorised it about a year ago but he said that as we'd pegged prices for a year we couldn't afford to give them a discount as well, so the invoice was amended . . . '

'And then what happened?' Greer's face and voice were grim.

'Their accounts office got on the phone, but he refused to give them the discount. Things got quite heated from the sound of it, so they cancelled their contract. Mr Hicks said we weren't making enough of a profit on it anyway, so it was no loss.'

'Did he indeed. And what about the Boat Show? We weren't giving them a discount. How did he manage to lose that account?' She was deceptively calm.

'He said the food we were supplying was too high a quality for an event like that — '

'He what?' Greer half rose from her seat, her eyes ablaze.

'He said they only wanted fast food and it didn't have to be the kind of ingredients we usually use. Nearly caused a walk-out in the kitchens.' She paused, wondering if it was wise to convey the rest of the staff's discontent to her employer. After all, Miss Jameson and Mr Hicks were, well, close, and everyone knew theirs was more than a business relationship.

Greer closed her eyes. A great weariness had overtaken her. This was all she needed — to return to find Steve had been meddling to an extent far beyond his responsibilities.

'Go on, Rosanna. What happened in the kitchens? Tell me the worst.'

'Instead of supplying our own make quiches and pizzas he said it was more economic to buy them in, and they had to cut down on the salads, and increase the potatoes and rice.'

'God help me,' Greer moaned. 'So they cancelled us for next year?'

'I'm sorry,' Rosanna nodded despairingly.

'It's not your sympathy I need at present, though I'm grateful for your loyalty.' Greer's eyes snapped open. 'Where's Mr Hicks now?'

'He's usually here by now — oh.' The door had swung open to admit a blond-haired man in a well-cut navy suit and striped shirt. 'Mr Hicks!'

'Greer — I wasn't expecting you!'

'Thank you, Rosanna. I'll buzz you when I need you.' As soon as the girl had gone, Greer looked at Steven. 'I understand I'm sitting in your seat.'

'Huh? No — don't be silly, that's your chair. I'll — er — use my old office, next to accounts.'

'Yes. I understand you've been keeping accounts busy, reissuing invoices.'

'Has that girl been worrying you about trivialities so soon? Look, I'll catch up with you later and get you up to date — '

'No, don't go, Steve. Sit down.' Her voice brooked no refusal. 'There's a lot we have to discuss.'

He loosened his tie. 'Yes, I know. You went away to think things over. But I thought we'd talk about it over dinner. If you'd told me you were coming back early I'd have rearranged my schedule, but I'm busy tonight — '

'No, I don't want to discuss us. I want to know what's happening here.'

'We've had a few problems, but nothing I couldn't handle — '

'From what I've heard, they were problems created by *you*.'

'You know, that secretary of yours is far too partisan. Just because I don't do things exactly as you do — '

'Steven — for God's sake. You've lost me two of my best customers! What have you been up to in my absence? Are you trying to destroy me?'

'Calm down, Greer, you're getting hysterical. Destroy you? Of course not. Just improving profitability. The profit margin was too low on the Faber account.'

'That account was worth more than money! It was prestige, and contacts. They entertained all sorts of people and I've had more orders than I can recall from customers who've eaten with them. And it's been regular income. There's been a function nearly every week! But you, you had to fall out with Mr Faber. This company's run on goodwill, not the profit and loss account. That's how it prospered and how it will continue. If I have to go on bended knee to Mr Faber, I will.'

Steve stood at the plate-glass window,

looking out at the treetops in the park. 'That would make me look very stupid.'

'Is that all you care about? Are you on some kind of an ego-trip? What are you trying to prove?'

'You can't bear not to be the boss, can you?' he said in a low voice, but she shook her head vehemently.

'I was happy to leave the business in your hands. I should have realised, though, that you'd have an accountant's priorities, not a caterer's. So I suppose this whole mess is down to me. In my innocence I thought you'd just keep it turning over for me, smoothly and profitably.'

'But don't you see,' he wheeled round and leant his hands flat on her desk, his smoothly good-looking face anxious, 'you need to combine financial expertise with your flair for catering, if you're ever going to make serious money. That's why we make such a perfect partnership.'

'A perfect partnership? Is that what you're talking about? A kind of live-in business partnership?' A note of bitterness had crept into her voice. She remembered how Byron had warned her.

She'd trusted Steve, but now she could see he was only out for his own eventual financial benefit. 'It wasn't me you wanted, was it? It was the business. Do you know, Steve, you've never actually told me you love me?'

'Oh, don't give me all that romantic nonsense, Greer. You don't believe in it any more than I do. We suit each other very well. We both enjoy the challenge and the financial rewards and we're neither of us likely to get any emotional hang-ups about anyone else, so us being a couple is the ideal solution. Sharing our work and our home.'

He paused and his cool grey eyes examined her face her some sign of acknowledgement that what he'd said was true, but after a lengthy silence he continued. 'You'd already made up your mind, hadn't you, even before you found out about my 'misdemeanours' in your absence?'

Greer nodded. 'I'm sorry.' Her voice was husky. 'Perhaps I was the person you're describing before I went away, but I've discovered I do have feelings, and I'm a more emotional person than I'd realised.'

'Am I to gather that these feelings you're suddenly experiencing are nothing to do with me?' He could hardly hear her whispered affirmative. 'So what happens now? Do you want me out of your life altogether, or do we still have a 'strictly business' relationship?'

'So long as you're prepared to accept that you don't have any autonomy in running things. I need to be able to trust you, though I don't just at present.'

'There is an alternative.'

'What's that?' She looked up at him curiously, and wondered how she could have contemplated life with him. Over-ambitious, calculating and devious, she was just a pawn in an elaborate game he was playing.

'You could sell out to me. I've got someone interested in financing an expansion. This could be really big.'

'I don't think so. The business is all I have. It's my life.'

'Yes, well it certainly is now. You're on your own, Greer baby, and I hope you like it up there, at your big desk on the top floor.' He walked to the door and paused as he exited. 'Whatever it was that happened while you were away, it doesn't look as though it's going to make you any happier.' And he departed with a malicious grin.

'And to hell with you, too, Steven Hicks,' she muttered as she stabbed out a number on the phone. 'Hello, I'd like to speak to Mr Faber, please. It's Greer Jameson.' She examined her nails while she waited, deciding on a strategy — 'Hello? He's busy? I'll call again — ' But she was talking to herself as the girl had rudely replaced the receiver.

'I can't bear it, any of it, any more,' she screamed, and picking up the phone she flung it to the far corner of the room, bringing her secretary diving in at the door.

'Whatever was that noise?'

'That, Rosanna, was the sound of my world crashing around my ears.'

8

The only consolation about the day that ensued was that she had no time to think about her own, personal, hurt. The staff were up in arms about the treatment meted out to them by Steven. The customers, at least those to whom she managed to speak, were disgruntled, and the suppliers were upset about the fact that Steven had been trying to make them cut the costs of their goods.

All in all, he'd made a pretty good job of ruining the past two or three years' hard work.

She had no time, until she was finally back at her flat, to contact her mother who, as she was told when she'd called a staff meeting, had been home for a few days with 'flu. Although she was utterly exhausted, she decided to go and see her, and start building those bridges she'd promised herself in the faraway world of Wales.

Quickly, she changed into jeans and sweat-shirt, and drove to the tiny maisonette on the outskirts of London where her mother now lived. She was shocked when she saw her mother who, in her late forties, was usually carefully dressed and made-up, but today, struggling to the door to admit Greer, was white-faced and shaking, and dressed in a shabby dressing-gown.

'What's going on here?' Greer looked around her, seeing furniture with which she'd grown up, conscious of the less-than-warm atmosphere in the room. 'Why haven't you got the fire on? You look dreadful, mother. Have you called the doctor?' She felt appalled — and guilty.

'It's only the 'flu. You know what they're like. Tell you to go home and go to bed, drink plenty of fluid — '

'And keep warm,' Greer finished for her, and bent down to switch on the electric fire.

'I don't need that. Look, I've got a blanket I can wrap round me. I'm not cold.'

'Well, *I* am, and it can't be good for you to live in such a low temperature, even if you are wrapped up. What's the matter? Are you short of money?'

'I've got enough to get by, dear. It's just the future that worries me. What's going to happen when I can't work any more?' Greer looked down at her in shocked horror. For the first time, she saw her mother as a frail, middle-aged woman who faced an insecure future.

Greer bent down, kneeling on the floor, and took both her mother's white, cold hands in her own. 'You don't have to concern yourself with the future. I'll look after you, just like you looked after me. That's what families are all about.'

'Families,' her mother echoed. 'I never thought of us as a family. I felt you resented me, and thought I left you on your own deliberately; but I didn't really have a choice, you know, with your father dead and leaving me with nothing.'

'I know that now, mother. And if it's not too late, I want us to be closer. Do you think that's possible?'

She could see the startled pleasure in her mother's eyes, as blue as her own, if a little faded. 'Of course it's possible. Anything's possible, if you want it badly enough.'

Greer busied herself getting a meal for her mother and generally putting the flat straight, telling her about the problems she'd encountered on her return, some of which she already knew.

'So you've finished with Steve, then? I wouldn't have interfered, but he wasn't the one for you, dear. I could see you weren't in love with him.'

Greer neatly side-stepped that line of talk. She wasn't ready to tell her mother about Byron. Now, or, perhaps, ever. 'Why haven't you ever married again? I'm sure you must have had opportunities, and it would have made life easier, wouldn't it?'

'That wouldn't be a very good reason for getting married, would it? To make life easier? No, nobody else ever seemed to come up to scratch, after your father. He was quite a man, you know. Such a shame you never knew him, but you weren't even two years old when he died. As you say, I did have one or two 'offers' but I was worried about you then. You seemed to live in your own little world, and I didn't want to disturb it.'

'Don't make me feel even more guilty than I do already,' Greer protested. 'If you'd wanted to remarry, you shouldn't have let a selfish little girl stand in your way.'

'Obviously I didn't want to remarry badly enough. And you were no more selfish than the average child, so there's no call to feel guilty.'

'But I didn't even realise that you were struggling financially still. I don't even know what the company is paying you. I've been so wrapped up in myself, I just feel terrible,' Greer wailed. 'There have I been, complacently patting myself on the back for being such a success in life, when I've been a dismal failure. I seem to make a nonsense of all my relationships, so it must be my fault.'

They were sitting by the fire, and her mother gently stroked her shining hair. 'You've been very clever, darling, but you still have a lot to learn.'

When she at last fell into the comfort of her own bed, Greer would have given anything to have had Byron's arms around her. She only hoped Ailsa appreciated her good fortune, having not only Byron, but his son as well. Greer couldn't imagine any greater happiness.

But happiness was not a commodity that featured much in Greer's life over the next few weeks. She felt as though she was at war with the world. Clients had to be mollified, suppliers reasoned with, and staff placated. Her mother's health was slow to improve, probably due to neglect in the early stages of 'flu, so Greer had her admitted to a private hospital within close reach.

She was still assailed by guilt at the thought of her ignorance of her mother's situation, and determined to take positive steps to improve her life. For the moment, though, that had to wait.

Rosanna had somehow worked the oracle and persuaded Mr Faber to accept an invitation to lunch with Greer. 'I'll take him to a really expensive restaurant where the food's appalling. That'll make him appreciate us,' she told Rosanna with glee, and her secretary was reassured to see the old fighting spirit returning. For a while it had seemed as though some of the stuffing had been knocked out of her employer, and she'd often caught her gazing into space, doing nothing, which was totally out of character. There was something amiss, but, as usual, she said nothing about any personal problems to any of her staff, nor even to Steve, nowadays.

It had been noted, by Greer as well as the rest of the staff, that he spent an inordinate amount of time with Carmine, a glamorous creature with a mass of red-gold hair who decorated the reception area, but Greer's attitude to that developing relationship appeared to be one of complete indifference. She suspected it was only to induce jealousy on her part, but if so it failed dismally. There was only one woman on this earth of whom she would ever be jealous again.

But she tried not to think about that.

After a few weeks, when things had settled down a little, she decided it was time to restructure the salary scales — with her mother very much in mind — and she called Steven into her office for that purpose. It was while they were thus engaged that she heard a commotion in the outside office.

'She's in conference — ' Rosanna's voice was heard raised in anger, but the door burst open with a crash.

'She's always in conference, or out

with a client, or tied up at a meeting, or on the other line. What do I have to do to get to speak to you, Greer, book Wembley Stadium for a buffet?'

His presence seemed to fill the spacious office as he stood, his wild dark hair too long, as usual, his black beard positively bristling with barely contained fury, his classically cut herring-bone tweed coat emphasising the sheer size of the man.

'What — what are you doing *here*?' she could only gasp in amazement.

'Trying to talk to you. You don't answer your phone at home, you have a battalion of employees who guard you better than the President of the United States, and if I wait for *you* to contact *me* we'll both be old and grey by then.'

'Oh, Byron,' she said weakly, feeling her heart do a jig of its own. 'There's nothing to talk about.'

'Not in front of him, there's not,' said Byron, rudely, frowning at Steve, who still sat unnecessarily close to Greer; had, in fact, drawn even closer at

Byron's dramatic entrance. 'Am I to gather that this is Steve?'

'Yes, it is. Steven Hicks, my accountant.'

'You have the advantage of me.' Steven was his smoothest and most polished self. 'I haven't the faintest idea who you might be.'

The two men looked at each other with mutual antagonism, and Greer didn't know whether to laugh or cry.

Neither of them really wanted *her*, yet they were glaring at each other like deadly rivals. Steven had needed her for her business acumen, and Byron for, well, for her body, that was what it boiled down to, after all.

'This is Byron Meredith,' she said, rather stiltedly. It was so strange to see Byron in this setting that, for once, she didn't feel in command of the situation. One never knew quite what Byron would do or say, and here she was used to being in control of just about everything and everyone.

'He was my landlord in Wales. He

owned the cottage I stayed in while I was away last month,' she added, at Steven's look of incomprehension.

'Aah. All is beginning to become clear. I had understood you were going to spend the month in solitary contemplation but . . . am I to understand that was not the case?'

Greer shot him a warning look, but he ignored her. Steven rarely displayed his true feelings, but she could tell by the firm set of his jaw and a nerve twitching in his cheek that he was angrier than he would ever let on.

'I mean, unless she didn't pay her rent — which I can't imagine to be the case — why on earth would one's landlord come rushing up to town, and burst into the room like a madman? Did she leave without saying goodbye, Byron? She's like that. Doesn't give a good goddamn, in truth. But you'll find that out for yourself.'

'Shut up, Steven. This has nothing to do with you. Rosanna — isn't that your phone ringing itself silly out there?'

Greer stood up, gathering her bag and gloves. Whatever it was Byron wanted to say to her, it had to be well away from here; and if she didn't give him the opportunity, she suspected he wouldn't have any hesitation in making such a scene that she'd be forced to do as he wished. If Steven was angry, Byron was barely holding down a volcano that was due for imminent eruption.

'I'll be out for lunch for the next — '

' — two hours,' Byron interrupted, and grabbing her hand he almost dragged her from the room, leaving Steven, Rosanna and the rest of the staff to gape in astonishment at such cavalier treatment.

'What is this all about?' she asked, once she was safely seated opposite him at a small Italian trattoria around the corner from the office. Her heart was still pounding painfully, but whether it was from the pell-mell pace at which he'd rushed her out of the building or the shock of seeing him she couldn't decide. Whatever, she knew her face was pink, her hair had tumbled from its chignon and the top two buttons of her prim, Victorian-styled, ruffle-necked blouse had come undone in the mêlée.

'You look wonderful,' he said, apropos of nothing at all, leaning forward, his dark blue eyes alight with pleasure. 'I've been trying to convince myself all these weeks that I was deluding myself. That you're not the most delectable creature that ever walked God's earth. But you are!'

'Byron, what is this all about? Why are you here?' She was determined to keep both feet on the ground, however difficult that might prove.

'Because you just left, without a word. I went to the cottage that evening, to talk to you, to try to explain things, but you'd gone. It was terrible. The cottage seemed even more desolate than — before.' For a moment the jubilation at having recaptured her deserted him.

'I'm sorry, Byron, but it was just as

painful for me.' The image of Ailsa and the small boy came between them, as sharply as though they were actually there, in the restaurant. 'Something happened that made me realise that I meant very little to you, really. That it was just an episode in your life, what we had, and . . . and that wasn't enough, for me.' It was an admission that was hard to make.

'What happened? What are you talking about?' He took her hand again, and his grasp was warm and strong, as she remembered only too well.

'I went to the market that day, after I left your place. And I saw you there. With a woman. And a small boy. You didn't tell me you have a son, Byron. That he's Ailsa's son — that was Ailsa, wasn't it?'

There was a long silence, during which Byron waved the hovering waiter away. Neither of them were in the mood for eating.

'So, you left because you saw Ailsa and little Gethin, with me?' He broke the silence at last. 'I can't quite follow your logic. You knew about Ailsa — I told you I was going to marry her. So why should seeing her make you take off without a word? Didn't you believe she existed until you actually saw her?'

'Oh yes, I believed she existed,' said Greer, bitterly. 'You made it clear to me when I first moved into the cottage that there was someone in your life, someone you wanted to move into the cottage. OK, so she was a shadowy figure until I saw her in the flesh, but what you hadn't said was how badly she'd been injured in the crash. Or that — she'd had your child. I hadn't realised until that moment just how much responsibility you had for her, how inextricably bound up your lives are with each other. It made me feel so bad, having wanted so much to come between you, to steal you away from her, if you like,' she gave a shaky laugh as though to minimise the way she felt, 'that I had to get away. Her need of you is even greater than mine. It's as simple as that.'

'I wish that it were.' Byron sighed deeply. 'I should have explained the whole thing to you sooner, but there never seemed to be the right time. That morning — after you'd stayed with me — I could see that you were hurting, that you were puzzled — but, selfishly, I didn't want to spoil things. I thought I could go on seeing you, at least until you came back to London, and that it would all work out somehow. I just wasn't thinking straight. Never could, when you were around.'

He looked around and beckoned the waiter. 'I think we should eat something, if only to stop them all looking at us so anxiously. They might ask us to leave otherwise!'

'Si, signor.' The waiter stood, pen poised.

'Just bring us some antipasto and a small carafe of house white for now. Oh — sorry. Will that be all right for you? I always forget — '

Greer nodded, smiling despite herself. It was nice to be treated as a helpless female again.

His face grave and thoughtful, Byron began to explain. 'I should have told you about Ailsa's injuries, I suppose — though that never seemed relevant. She's learnt to live with them, but I still feel responsible. Always will. She used to love to ride, to walk over the mountains, play tennis — all those things. But now she can't. As for Gethin — what makes you so certain he's my son?'

'Don't be ridiculous! He's the spitting image of you. I've never seen a child so like its father. You're not denying that you are, surely?'

'I know that I'm not,' he said, softly, his eyes holding hers. 'He's my brother's son. Ailsa was Liam's wife.'

Greer stared at him in dazed incomprehension.

That would account for the close resemblance. Byron leant forward, his eyes burning into her. 'He's not my son

— he's my nephew. Liam and I were like two peas out of the same pod, and little Gethin has all the same characteristics and colouring. Are you taking all this in, Greer?'

'Yes.' Her reply was so faint he could scarcely hear it against the clatter of plates, the clink of bottles and the hum of conversation in the restaurant. 'And Ailsa was your brother's wife? Is your brother's widow?' She was so taken aback at this revelation, her mind was in a whirl.

'That's right. They'd only been married a couple of years when the accident happened. They were living at the cottage by then, just planning how to renovate it — when he died.'

'Then why did you want her to go back there? You said — a lifetime ago when we first met — that you wanted someone to move in there. That someone was Ailsa, wasn't it?' The waiter arrived with a dish of hors d'oeuvres, discreetly poured the wine and left them to what was obviously a very traumatic conversation. 'Why should she want to move back, after what happened there?'

'To make sure the past was well and truly behind her, she said. To prove that she could live with it before she went forward into the future.'

'With you?'

'Yes. I asked her to marry me.'

'You fell in love with her? When? After Liam died, or before?' Greer felt cold all over and knew that she couldn't eat even a morsel of the food that had been put in front of her.

'Of course not — not before. Not even after, not really. I am — devoted to her. We've shared so much . . . our grief . . . bringing up Gethin . . . running the farm.'

'You're marrying her, but you don't love her?' Greer insisted on knowing.

'I told you — I'm devoted to her. But I don't love her in the way I now know I could feel. I owe it to her, Greer; if it hadn't been for me . . . ' His eyes were tormented, begging her to understand.

'So that's what you meant by taking on all his responsibilities. Not only the farm, but his wife and son as well?' Greer cried out, horrified at the sacrifice, at the waste, at the wrongness of it all.

'Yes. And I'm not going back on it, no matter what.'

'Then why, oh why, did you come chasing up here to see me? I'd got used to living with the pain, but now I think it'll be even worse. Knowing — '

'Knowing that I don't love Ailsa? Do you think it's any easier for me? If I'd known it was possible — if I'd even suspected — that I'd ever meet someone, someone I'd care about, then I would have thought twice about offering Ailsa security and family life for Gethin. But it's too late now. I can't destroy her all over again, don't you see?'

'Oh, yes, I can see all right.' Greer couldn't prevent the note of bitterness creeping into her voice. 'So what was the point of seeing me again? Did you think we'd carry on where we left off? That you could visit me in London and my flat could be our little love-nest. That you'd have a nice, grateful wife but you could carry on having an affair with me?'

Angrily, she pushed her plate to one side and dashed the hot tears from her eyes.

'No, no, that's not what I want. I wanted to tell you why I couldn't offer you any more, and I also wanted to tell you how much you mean to me. To be honest, I didn't think you wanted anything more. Your life is here, any fool can see that. You've created a thriving business, and it's clear you enjoy what you're doing. What could I offer you? A boring life in a rural community?'

'I've never looked that far ahead. You've never given me any reason to believe it would last longer than a holiday. I had the shock of my life when you marched into the office. It was like seeing a ghost.'

'Some ghost.' Byron smiled bleakly. 'I

never could offer you a future. I just kept hoping that somehow things might come right in the end. A bit like a child who believes there really is a Santa Claus and he'll come up with the goodies, or that there really is a crock of gold at the end of the rainbow. Just dreams they were, I realise that now.'

'Yes, just dreams,' Greer echoed. 'And now you'll go back to Wales and I'll carry on with my life.'

'I can't tell you how bitterly I regret causing you pain. If only we'd never met — '

'No, don't say that. I'm *glad*,' she said, fiercely. 'You've changed me, and I think I'll probably be a nicer person now.' She managed a rather shaky laugh.

Somehow, they paid the bill, left the restaurant and returned, in body anyway, to the rest of the world. They walked, not talking, just gripping hands, through the clamorous streets till they found themselves in a park. Greer never knew, afterwards, which park it was, only that the almost-bare branches dripped on their heads, that the horizon was lost in a thin grey mist, and that they were alone.

They kissed frantically. They clung to each other like shipwreck victims. Because they both knew this was the end. She could never take him away from Ailsa. He would never go back on his word.

'Don't forget me,' he said at last, releasing her from the shelter of those all-enveloping arms, and she shook her head, beyond words, her eyes drowning in tears.

When she waved him farewell from her office steps it was as though her life was already over. She was doomed to loneliness and lovelessness for ever.

'Don't be such a fool,' she scolded herself, going up in the lift. 'You were reasonably happy before you met him, so why shouldn't you be again?'

But she knew she was only practising self-deceit.

9

'If you love him as much as you say you do, then you've got to fight for him.'

'Fight? Mother, I can't fight a woman who's been crippled in the accident which killed her husband. Who's been left with a fatherless baby and very little prospect of meeting anyone else who'd marry her.'

'Why? Just because she walks with a limp and has a child? What's to stop someone else falling in love with her? What does she think about it?'

'Ailsa?' Greer frowned. 'I don't know. Presumably as she accepted his proposal of marriage, she's happy with the situation.'

She'd collected her mother from the nursing home early on Sunday morning and they were sitting in the lounge of her mother's small maisonette, warmed by a new, more effective, heater Greer had installed, and eating the lunch she'd prepared. Over the past few days her mother had managed to extract the reason for Greer's deep unhappiness, and once the dam had been breached, Greer had poured out her heart.

But the balm of revelation only eased the pain momentarily, and Greer only toyed with the salad she'd prepared.

'Well, I think you should ask her. But that's just my opinion. Call me an interfering, meddling woman, if you like, but it simply isn't like you to give up so easily, and I think you should do something about it.'

'Give up easily? Is that what you think? It's the hardest thing I've ever done in my life. Not contacting Byron is like trying to stop breathing. I've sat and looked at the telephone for hours, willing myself *not* to pick it up, just to hear his voice. You don't know what it's like, mother.'

'On the contrary, I *do* know what it's like. It might have been a long time ago, but I know what losing the man you love means. Except, in your case, he's still alive, and where there's life there's hope!'

'I'm sorry — that was clumsy of me, wasn't it? Only thinking of myself again, aren't I? But what can I do, go and confront Ailsa, and tell her I'm in love with Byron, and I think he loves me back?'

'Yes!' Her mother stood up, her old fighting spirit restored. Greer was beginning to discover from whom she had inherited her 'get up and go' and, to her eternal surprise, it was her mother. Given the same opportunities Greer had enjoyed, she would probably have achieved even more. 'I'll come with you if you want some Dutch courage!'

'Drive to Wales now, you mean?' Greer looked up, her blue eyes startled.

'Well, we're both back at work tomorrow, aren't we, so why not now?'

Greer looked at her watch. 'We could be there about five o'clock. But I don't know where she'll be. She may have moved into the cottage — '

'Stop being so indecisive, it's out of character. We'll find her. You owe it to yourself and Byron, but most of all you owe it to her. How would you like someone to marry you out of duty and pity?'

* * *

They crossed the Severn Bridge at four o'clock and a watery sun turned the scattered leaves to a bronzed gold. It glistened on tumbling rivers and lit up great swathes of the hillsides, leaving other slopes in deep shadow.

Greer felt her trepidation turned to a calm certainty that what she was doing was right. After all, Ailsa should know the score. Then it would be her decision, but a decision based on knowledge. Even so, the flutter at the base of her stomach made Greer wonder if she'd have the courage once she faced her.

'However did you find the place?' her

mother wondered as they wove their way through the twisting narrow lanes. 'It really is the back of beyond.'

Leaves danced all around them as Greer drove swiftly towards the cottage. In London she'd hardly been aware of the seasons, but here autumn had arrived with a vengeance, with mellow colours and a profusion of berries on otherwise bare branches. Everything seemed ripe and opulent, and the air was still and heavy.

She rounded the last bend before the cottage, her pulses racing. Suppose Byron was there, with Ailsa? Suppose he'd lied? Suppose he really did love Ailsa and had only told her otherwise to soothe her wounded pride?

'Here we are,' she said grimly, as she braked to a halt in the drive, and noted, nervously, that a lamp had been lit in the living-room against the gathering gloom.

'I'll wait here, that's best,' said her mother. 'But I'll be here if you need me.'

'I don't think she'll attack me,' Greer tried to joke, but her face was stiff with apprehension.

Ailsa came to the door before she'd even knocked, and looked at her calmly.

'You don't know me. I stayed here . . . in September.' How on earth was she going to broach the subject?

'Oh . . . yes, I remember. Come in — I was just making some tea.' She stood aside and Greer went in with a pang of remembered happiness. The hall had been redecorated and was light and bright in soft yellow and grey.

'So, you came back.' Ailsa set down the tray before the fire and glanced at her curiously. 'Were you in the neighbourhood, or did you come back for something? You didn't leave anything here, did you?'

Only my heart, Greer wanted to say. 'No. As a matter of fact,' taking a deep breath, 'I wanted to talk to you.' She felt she must be very pale.

'To me? What on earth for? How do you even know who I am?' She seemed so gentle and genuinely puzzled that Greer felt like a criminal.

'I wanted to talk to you about — Byron.' Greer's hand shook and the cup rattled in its saucer.

'About Byron.' This time her look was long and hard, and then she nodded as if to herself. 'Yes. I'm beginning to understand.'

'He tells me that you're getting married.' Ailsa watched her without speaking. 'He explained that you were married to his brother, that you have a little boy, and that he asked you to marry him after his brother died.'

'Yes, that's all true. Why did you want to talk to me?'

'I wanted to know — how you felt about it?' Greer blurted out, and her face went from white to scarlet. 'If you must know, I want to know if you love him.'

'Because you do?'

'Yes.' She looked down at her hands, which were tied in knots. 'Very much.'

'I see. Mm, yes I do understand now.'

'Oh, Ailsa — I don't want to hurt you, but I think you should know, otherwise it's not fair; for you, or me, or even Byron; is it?'

'Does he know you're here?' At Greer's quick shake of the head she smiled briefly. 'No, of course not. I have to be protected, at all costs. He treats me as though I'm some kind of separate species, not flesh and blood with my own thoughts and feelings. This was all his idea, you know, that we should marry.'

'But you accepted, didn't you?'

'Yes. I was very vulnerable at the time; and then, having accepted, it seemed to relieve his conscience so much that I've never been able to talk it over with him, to discuss whether or not it was such a good idea.'

A tiny spark of hope began to flare inside Greer. What was Ailsa saying, that perhaps she had reservations about the marriage?

'You mean — you're not altogether certain that you want to marry Byron?'

Ailsa paused for thought, gazing into the leaping firelight. 'At first, it seemed the ideal solution. It took me a very long time to recover from Liam's death, and I honestly thought I never would. Byron was wonderful to Gethin, and he came to look on him almost as his father. It seemed a logical conclusion. There was only one thing that troubled me.' She looked up, her soft hazel eyes full and frank on Greer's. 'We weren't in love. It was more or less a marriage of convenience.'

'But you're going to go through with it?'

She hesitated. 'I was going to. I wanted to come back here, to make sure all my ghosts have been laid, and they have. But lately, Byron's been different. Edgy. Even more concerned, if anything, with my welfare. And yet it's been as though he's been trying not to get irritable with me. He's always had quite a temper, though since the accident he's never shown it when I've been around; but I've had the feeling that it's only just been under control. Now I know why.'

'You do?'

'Because of you. I could almost tell you to the day when you arrived in his life. Let me think — somewhere around the beginning of September? Was that when you arrived?'

'Yes — but we fought like cat and dog at first. It wasn't until towards the end of my stay that we began to get . . . involved.'

'Don't you believe it. You came into his life like a thunderbolt, and he's never recovered.' To Greer's astonishment, Ailsa was smiling.

'And you don't mind?'

'Shall I tell you something that may astonish you? It's a relief — a vast relief. I've been so worried, knowing it was wrong, that I shouldn't use Byron as a kind of bolt-hole, and yet I didn't know how to tell him.'

'Then you'll release him? You don't want to marry him?' She wanted to jump up and dance around the room.

'Sounds a bit dramatic, doesn't it? Release him. He's not in prison, after all.'

'I think it may have been a kind of prison for him. He certainly felt bound to do what he thought was the right thing for you and the boy.'

'Yes, he's a wonderful man, and I suppose I'm mad, letting him slip through my fingers. But you can't dictate who you'll fall in love with, can you? And I'm not in love with him, I'm afraid.' She said it a shade regretfully, and Greer felt a pang of remorse. She had, after all, just altered the course of this woman's life.

'You are sure about this, aren't you? I mean, it's not a spur of the moment thing, is it?'

'No. As I said, it's been troubling me a lot lately, wondering what to do, and now you've pushed me in the right direction.'

'But what do you think Byron will say, when he finds out that we've been conspiring together? That I came here to talk to you?'

Ailsa covered her mouth with her hand in mock horror, but her eyes were laughing. 'We'll both have to pretend to be helplessly feminine about this,' she giggled, 'and that'll leave him in utter confusion.'

'Oh, Ailsa. I really am throwing myself at him, aren't I? Supposing he doesn't want me, not on a permanent basis, anyway?'

'Well, that's a problem for the two of you to sort out. With me out of the way, at least you only have each other to consider. I don't know what either of you wants, but I just hope you'll both be happy. Byron deserves it.'

'And so do you, Ailsa. So do you. Listen, can I bring my mother in for a cup of tea before she faints for lack of sustenance out there?'

Greer was ushering her mother indoors when a neighbour arrived, bringing with her Ailsa's son. He greeted Ailsa with rapturous descriptions of the party he'd just attended, presenting her with a somewhat sticky bag of sweets and a large red balloon.

Greer, who never before had experienced even a twinge of maternal instincts, could hardly take her eyes off the small boy, entranced by his huge vividly blue eyes and the mop of tangled curls. He would glance at her shyly now and then, out of the corners of those amazing eyes, as if aware of her unusual interest in him, and she smiled at him in delight.

For the first time in what seemed like aeons, she was light-hearted and — almost — happy. There was only one, very large, cloud on her particular horizon: Byron's reaction to his 'broken engagement', when he learnt about it, and what his plans for the future might hold. Perhaps, even without Ailsa in the picture, she still didn't feature in those plans. After all, he'd bade her farewell pretty decisively, and perhaps he hadn't found it that difficult, being without her.

What would she say, what would she

do, if he rejected her?

As if reading her thoughts Ailsa murmured to her 'Byron will be at the farm now, if you want to go and find him,' her dark eyes sympathetic and concerned, and Greer was astonished at such generous-heartedness from someone she'd assumed to be her rival.

'Yes, I suppose I'd better summon up my courage and go and tackle him,' she acknowledged, already feeling nervous at the thought. 'Would you mind if my mother stays here, with you? I think this is something I have to do alone.'

The night was dark as pitch with a wind beginning to get up a blow, denuding the trees of what leaves remained. It was not an auspicious night to be seeking out one's lover.

The Jensen was parked in the courtyard, but when Greer poked her head around the office door, she found it in darkness.

'Looking for the boss?' a young lad, walking past called. 'You'll find him down there, it's evening stables,' he explained, though Greer had no idea what he meant. She walked to the far end of the courtyard and through a gate into the stableyard.

Pools of light were thrown from the open tops of the stable doors and she could hear the clanking of buckets as some of the horses ate, whilst others whinnied and snickered, awaiting the arrival of their feed. The stable lads busied themselves, whistling as they went, and the air was filled with the sweet smell of good hay and well-groomed horses.

This was Byron's world.

She could see him leaning over the top of a stable door, lost in thought, and she crossed quietly to him in her moon-boots.

'Byron?'

He turned so swiftly that he startled the horse and she heard him skitter in alarm, saw the toss of his mane as he looked to see the cause of his master's sudden action. Byron could only stare at her as though struck dumb.

In the pale beam of light she watched his expression change from a flare of delight, through bafflement to quick anger.

'What are you doing here?' he cried in seeming anguish. 'Do you get some kind of a kick out of tormenting me? You've got to stay out of my life, for good.'

She stepped back as though she'd been struck.

'I had to come. I had to speak to Ailsa,' she cried defiantly and he took a menacing step towards her.

'You *what?*' His eyes blazed even in the fading light.

'It wasn't fair — to her — not to know you were marrying her for all the wrong reasons.' Greer faltered as he looked as though he was about to use physical violence. 'No, listen to me, Byron! We talked, about you, about us, about her and — '

'Come into the office.' His voice was sheet ice. 'We can't talk out here.'

She was vaguely aware that the stable

lads were showing great interest in the conversation, and she followed Byron's broad unforgiving back across the yard.

'What did you say to her?' he asked, once they faced each other again in the bright fluorescent light of the office. He was making a visible effort to keep his temper under control.

'I can't remember exactly — I was so worked up about it all. But she's stronger than you think, Byron. She realises that she turned to you when she needed help, but now she can make it on her own.'

He shook his head obstinately. 'You shouldn't have interfered. She obviously only said what she thought you wanted to hear. She's like that.'

'No, that's not true! She's been worried lately about the fact that it seemed wrong. The truth is that she's been wondering how to break it off with you, but didn't know how.'

He stared at her wildly. 'I don't believe you. She's depended on me completely, she and Gethin.'

'Yes, she has. But she doesn't want to do that for the rest of her life. She doesn't love you, any more than you love her. Not the kind of love that marriage should be based on, anyway. If you don't believe me, ask her yourself,' she finished, hurt and bewildered by his reaction.

Slowly, Byron sank down onto the edge of a desk, his brow creased. 'Did you tell her — about us?' he asked, at last, looking up from under his dark brows. 'Did you tell her that we'd been lovers?'

She flinched from the cold way he said it. He seemed only concerned about Ailsa, and not at all about her own feelings. Icy fingers of fear traversed her spine. If she had misjudged him, if he didn't really care . . .

She shook her head, wordlessly, and he continued to study her, his eyes, for once, expressionless.

'And she really said that she doesn't want to marry me? That she thinks it was a big mistake?' At her silent assent he took a deep shuddering breath, then stood up straight and stretched, as though a huge burden had been lifted from him.

'Well, that lets me off the hook then, doesn't it?'

She looked at him, startled at his change of mood. She was wary of him, though she could see that the set of his jaw had softened.

'Off the hook?' she echoed, faintly.

'Yes. I don't have to get married. I was angry with you for meddling, and afraid you'd hurt Ailsa, who I wouldn't hurt for the world. But if she doesn't want to get married — not to me, at any rate — then I'm free. For the first time for years, I can do exactly as I please.'

'So what will you do?' She tried to swallow but her throat was constricted.

'Do? Pick up the threads of my happy bachelor days, I suppose — '

Before she could listen to any more, Greer turned and fled. She charged out of the office, crashing the door to behind her, and jumped into her car.

With a quick flick of her shaking fingers she turned on the ignition, then screeched into reverse, sliding on the gravel, pushed it into gear and shot out of the yard.

She didn't know where she was going, only that she had to get away.

She drove furiously, this way and that, until the narrow track she was on finally ran out of road halfway up a mountain. She switched off the engine and sat in the total silence only to be found in the depths of the countryside on a slightly foggy night.

Her worst fears had been confirmed. He'd told her he was to marry Ailsa. But he'd never said he wanted to marry her. Or that she would feature in any permanent way in his future. He had accepted that she would return to London, and that would be an end to it.

She'd been fooling herself. Had assumed the fierce, all-consuming love she felt for him was reciprocated.

All she'd succeeded in doing was giving him back his freedom. According to all reports, he'd made full use of that before, and no doubt would do so again.

She was just the first of another long line of fresh conquests.

She sat there until the warm interior of the car grew chill, and the windows were misted inside as well as out. It was getting late, and she and her mother had to get back to London.

With a weariness more of mind and spirit than of body, she drove slowly away, back to the cottage to collect her mother.

But the Jensen was parked in the driveway.

Had he gone to persuade Ailsa to change her mind?

Dispiritedly, she walked to the door and, finding it unlatched, went in, to be confronted by a cosy domestic scene, with Byron bouncing Gethin on his knee while talking animatedly to her mother. Ailsa, to Greer's surprise, had picked up some tapestry work and was serenely embroidering.

Greer walked into the room and met Byron's eyes sourly.

'Good, you're back. We were getting worried about you!'

'Oh, really. Doesn't look as though I've been missed at all. Come on, mother, it's time we were off, or we won't be back by midnight.' She was stiff with misery, made even more stark by the apparent contentment of everyone else in the room.

But Byron was standing, handing her mother the sleepy-eyed little boy. 'Look after him a minute,' he smiled, his ill-temper apparently having completely evaporated, 'while I talk to Greer.'

As though anticipating refusal, he grasped her elbow firmly and almost pushed her from the room, but once in the narrow hallway she hissed, 'We've nothing to talk about.'

Still he propelled her along, into the kitchen, which was warmed by a spanking new scarlet Aga, until she reached the barrier of the pine table which still stood in the middle of the room.

Turning her round, none too gently, he placed his hands, palms down, on either side of her. She had no way to go. She could only glare at him in defiance.

'You know that corny line they always say in films — God, but you're beautiful when you're angry?' he began, unexpectedly, his full lower lip twitching with amusement. 'It's true! In your case anyway.'

'What do you want with me, Byron? I told you I have to get back to London, and it's a bit foggy tonight, so I don't want to hang about — '

'Why *are* you so angry?' He totally ignored what she'd just said.

'Why . . . ? You must be about as sensitive as — as this table.' She gripped its edge with her fingers, to prevent them from either hitting him, or caressing that wonderful face, so close to her own. If only he'd loved her as she loved him, then she wouldn't be in this torment. 'You made it very plain that I don't figure in your life at all, that you were pleased to have your 'freedom' again. Well — go ahead. I hope you enjoy it.'

His scrutiny was intense and she could feel herself flushing as those magnetic eyes lingered on her eyes, her mouth, then travelled indolently down. Her entire body grew warm under his intense gaze.

The familiar aroma of potent cologne, and wool, and horses, and damp soft air invaded her senses. 'Please let me go, Byron,' she whispered, needing to escape from the prison of his arms. Though they weren't touching her, they formed a barrier as impenetrable as thorns, because she dare not touch him. She wanted to push him away. To run. To flee. To escape from the pain of a love that wasn't returned.

'Why should I let you go?' His voice was husky.

'Because — because you don't love me.'

'It's very obvious you never had an older brother,' he said, unexpectedly and, startled into a careless action, she looked up into his eyes. They glittered beneath the dark brows, and she was mesmerised.

'What do you mean?' she managed to whisper.

'You're not used to being teased. Did you really think I was serious about being free — about 'picking up the threads' of my bachelor days?'

Greer swallowed hard and nodded, her eyes still transfixed by his.

Slowly, Byron shook his head, looking at her as though she was a demented child. 'It's a terrible thought — but I'll never be free again. Loving you the way I do, you've got me in chains, don't you know that, you silly goose?'

'No, no. I thought — I thought — I'd been so afraid, you see, that you didn't mean what you said. I couldn't wait to hear any more. My worse fears had been realised, when you looked so happy to be free of your commitment to Ailsa.'

'I was happy — and I'm even happier now I've had a chance to talk to her about it. It was very presumptuous of me, to assume that I was the only answer to her problems. Apparently she's met someone, a solicitor from Hereford. They've only seen each other a couple of times, but that old black magic — the chemistry of mutual attraction — seems to be operating. And even if nothing comes of it, she says she'd rather be on her own than ruin both our lives — and possibly yours as well.'

He paused, and a small frown creased his brow. 'There's only one problem now. How the devil will you, a successful urban businesswoman, take to burying herself in the country?'

'Burying myself?' Greer looked dazed.

'Yes, well, if we're going to be

married, I had assumed that you'd actually be moving down here, with me.'

'Married?'

'Stop repeating everything I say like a rather faint echo from the mountains, and pull yourself together. What happened to that supremely confident young woman who overwhelmed me when we first met? Why've you crumpled to bits like this?'

'I don't know. I've never been in love before. P'raps this is how it affects me.' She could feel tension flooding from her, as her fingers loosened their hold on the wooden table and began to creep up the thick soft wool of his sweater.

'Oh God, I hope not. I much prefer the wild-cat you were before. I do like a good fight to keep me on my toes now and then.' His hands encircled her waist.

'Do you indeed? Well, once I've recovered my equilibrium I'll no doubt revert to type.' The corners of her mouth began to lift.

'That's more like the Greer I know and love. To be serious for a moment, though, my darling — how *will* you take to living down here? What about your business?'

'Oh that's easy. Steve said he's found someone who wants to put money into it, as his partner — '

'You won't sell out to Steve, will you? I mean, that business has been like your baby, and I don't think he'd care for it as you have.'

'Of course not! But if he's got someone interested, obviously it's a good commercial proposition, so I should be able to find someone as a 'sleeping partner' and I'll put my mother in to run things. She'll love the challenge — I've discovered she's just as pushy as I am.' She laughed up into his eyes, her own glowing with unalloyed happiness.

'I don't believe you — nobody could be that bad,' he teased as his lips descended and they clung to each other as though they were assuaging the thirst of countless years, their mouths performing a lustful coupling of their own.

Byron's hands wrought their own special magic on her eager body as he caressed her with an almost painful tenderness until they drew back, breathless, from one another.

'There's only one thing,' he kissed the tip of her nose, 'that you haven't told me.' His lips trailed across the peach bloom of her cheek. 'And that's,' he nuzzled her brow where tendrils of pale hair clung, 'if you'll marry me.'

'I once thought I was wishing for the moon, wanting you,' she admitted, stroking the curled hair of his beard. 'But now it's mine, and so are you.'

'For ever and ever?' he whispered.

'Till death us do part.'

THE END

Other titles in the Linford Romance Library:

CONVALESCENT HEART

Lynne Collins

They called Romily the Snow Queen, but once she had been all fire and passion, kindled into loving by a man's kiss and sure it would last a lifetime. She still believed it would, for her. It had lasted only a few months for the man who had stormed into her heart. After Greg, how could she trust any man again? So was it likely that surgeon Jake Conway could pierce the icy armour that the lovely ward sister had wrapped about her emotions?

TOO MANY LOVES

Juliet Gray

Justin Caldwell, a famous personality of stage and screen, was blessed with good looks and charm that few women could resist. Stacy was a newcomer to England and she was not impressed by the handsome stranger; she thought him arrogant, ill-mannered and detestable. By the time that Justin desired to begin again on a new footing it was much too late to redeem himself in her eyes, for there had been too many loves in his life.

MYSTERY AT MELBECK

Gillian Kaye

Meg Bowering goes to Melbeck House in the Yorkshire Dales to nurse the rich, elderly Mrs Peacock. She likes her patient and is immediately attracted to Mrs Peacock's nephew and heir, Geoffrey, who farms nearby. But Geoffrey is a gambling man and Meg could never have foreseen the dreadful chain of events which follow. Throughout her ordeal, she is helped by the local vicar, Andrew Sheratt, and she soon discovers where her heart really lies.